I0603605

Vampire

Starlight Investigations - Book 2

Marnie Atwell

One

The portal that linked Earth with the planet, Mystique, shimmered in the twilight. As the connection strengthened, the outside of the doorway began to sparkle in the same colour blue as a late afternoon's sky. Tendrils developed from the frame and wound their way towards the centre, moving through the colour spectrum from blue to pink. Two visitors breached the surface and set foot upon the Earth.

The first to arrive was Adair, Queen of the Battle Stars, an elegant woman dressed in a warrior's uniform worn by the Royals. Her ruby coloured jacket was made of a material similar in looks and feel to leather, which acted like a second skin, able to adapt itself to the wearer. It had a collar that protected the back of the neck and base of the skull, and lowered to a V neck at the front, finishing at the base of her ribcage. Gold etchings followed the neckline and finished at the waistline. Her pants were jet black and crafted from the same material as her jacket. Ruby boots, that rose halfway up her shins, adorned her feet.

Her long, white hair had been fashioned into a classic roll with her fringe feathering across her forehead, creating a softness to her features. The apricot coloured jewel shaped like a diamond, sat in the middle of her forehead. It was pretty much the only part of her crown that could be seen. The rest had been craftily hidden beneath her hair. Her mauve coloured lips were set in a straight line and her bright blue eyes flashed between anger and resignation as she gazed upon the creature she had travelled with.

Sarina, Queen of the Vampires, glared back. Her long, black hair was tucked behind her petite, pointy ears. Her blood-red eyes had a predatory feel to them and caused Adair to shift slightly in her stance. A slow, malicious smile spread across Sarina's face, making her appear even creepier than before. Her greyish-blue skin was supple and did not crease at all as her facial features changed.

She wore a dress made from navy blue satin inlaid with navy blue lace, short in the front and long in the back. It had long sleeves and a V neck line. Sarina had teamed this with a brown, leather corset that tied at the front and sat below her breast line. The waistline was shaped to a V giving her body a very feminine appearance. Black stockings with suspenders were worn beneath black boots with a three inch heel.

Adair casually moved her eyes away from Sarina to perform a sweep of the area. She was pleased to find there were no humans within their vicinity. She returned her gaze to Sarina to provide her with the rules one more time before letting her loose amongst the human race.

"You have one week to find a mate and be back at the portal, or the implant in your chest will explode. The Battle Stars, who are called Gatherers here, are off limits. You are forbidden to harm them in any way, but you can have as many humans as you want."

"That was not the deal, Adair," Sarina began, folding her arms in anger and circling the Queen. "Yes, I agreed to leave *most* of your Battle Stars alone, even as they hunt me to bring me back to your prison. There was no discussion with regards to the amount of time I had on Earth.

"For three thousand years we lived on your planet, under protest, but in peace. It was your Battle Stars that broke the rules and killed my husband, Karayan, therefore it will be one of your Battle Stars that replaces him. I have given you the name of the one I want. If you have brought me to his location, the transformation will be quick and I will call on you to return before the week has passed. If you have not, then I will be here as long as it takes for me to find him. I make this promise to you; the devastation to the human race will be considerable and the blame will lie on your head if you have not kept up your end of the bargain."

"I have already apologised for the loss of Karayan. I am going above and beyond my duties in bringing you here and allowing you to infect one of my best warriors," Queen Adair responded.

Sarina laughed, "You have brought me here in an attempt to appease my anger. You are frightened of my wrath and what my kind are capable of doing to your pathetic Battle Stars. Every single one of them has the perfect DNA sequence to become one of us. One bite from us, a drop of our blood and a human sacrifice is all it would take to turn your warriors into the perfect killing machines entirely under our control.

"Vampires know when their makers are dead, and as I am the maker of each and every one of my children on your planet, you would have a hard time containing them all after they were set free from my bonds. So you see, Adair, you were never in control and you will wait for my call before returning for me. The device that you believe is in my chest is actually in one of your guardians. Now, what was her name? Oh yes, Karah. I placed it there myself two weeks ago during her visit to my land. Now tell me, how far away is my new mate?"

"He is one and a half thousand kilometres south. There are only two portals located in this country. One on the Eastern side, which is where we are now and the other is on the Western side."

"That is too far for the fairies that call to him to feel my presence!" she roared in frustration.

"The hunt for you has begun already. A Locator will have picked you up on their radar and contacted their first available Gatherer as we speak. When you have contact with that Gatherer, drop your name and mine. They will call their superiors for instructions and I will be contacted. I will make sure that your target crosses your path, after all, it is in my planet's best interest."

"I didn't think you had it in you to sacrifice one of your own," Sarina said with a surprised inflection in her voice.

"The lives of the many outweigh the lives of the few," Adair said sadly.

"Thanks for the lift. I think it's time you got back to ruling your planet, hey. I will be bringing back an extremely hungry vampire. You had better ensure there are plenty of *healthy* humans in stock to quench his thirst," Sarina ordered.

Adair was totally frustrated at being out-manoeuvred by the beast. She walked to the portal with her head held high even though her self-esteem had taken a battering. Without a backwards glance, she stepped through the portal on Earth and exited the portal at the castle in her kingdom.

If what Sarina had said was true, Adair would need to locate Karah and get her to the Restorers as quickly as possible. Only they would be able to remove the device without any harm coming to her most trusted guardian.

Sarina decided she should head east until she hit the coastline and then travel south. She liked the feel of the forest that housed the portal. The trees were taller than the ones on Mystique, and were clumped more closely together, giving the area a cosier feel. She weaved her way towards the ocean without concern until the landscape began to change. Sarina found herself in the suburbs, which was unlike anything she had experienced before.

VAMPIRE

There were orbs of light that glowed mysteriously in the air, casting out the shadows. Some of them were white, while others produced an orange light. They were definitely not fire, and Sarina felt herself becoming a little afraid. The next thing she noticed was the solid structures that were positioned in lines across the landscape. Sarina approached cautiously and realised they were dwellings for the humans, as the smell of blood reached her nasal passages.

The humans had obviously become better at protecting themselves from the elements in her absence. She wondered if the prey on Mystique were also given dwellings such as these to live in, whilst they were not trapped in her land providing a blood donation to her family. While the smell of them woke her hunger, Sarina was very old and highly disciplined. The night was young and there would be plenty of time to drink later. She could go for weeks without feeding and still remain strong. Drinking nightly was a luxury, not a necessity.

The number of dwellings indicated there had been an explosion in human population. A flash of anger ripped through her as she realised her kind were being kept away from their food source unnecessarily. If there were this many humans living in this one small section of the planet, then there must be more than enough humans to keep them fit and healthy for centuries. A noise to her right interrupted her ponderings. The reason for her visit was to bring the awareness of her presence to the Gatherers, not the humans. Besides, it was important that she found somewhere to base herself before dawn. After determining the noise was created by a small mammal, she continued on her journey.

A river of blackness lay across her path. She sniffed the air and screwed up her nose. The stuff smelled awful. She had nothing to compare it to and didn't know if it was dangerous or not. Sarina bent down and placed her finger on the substance. It was hard and unyielding. She pressed her hand on its surface then jumped when an unfamiliar sound suddenly blasted through the quiet.

A set of lights shone in her direction, bathing her in white light. Sarina cringed and spun her body away. The car rolled forward and veered left, following the dark river. The smell made her gag so she covered her face with her hand. Sarina stared at the vehicle with worry. She didn't know what it was and wondered why. They had learned a long time ago how to read memories through the blood of those they fed on. None of the memories she had gleaned showed her what that thing could be or the dark river in front of her. Sarina stood and bravely ran across the river of darkness. Even when she had made it to the other side safely, she didn't stop running. She had to get to the ocean.

The closer she got, the more buildings and black rivers she came across. Instead of the sprawling landscape she had come from, there were lights and tall, towering structures everywhere. She whimpered with fear but then took stock of herself. She was the Queen of the

Vampires. These were humans, her prey. She was more powerful than they would ever be, and they had never seen a creature like her in their lifetime. She kept to the shadows wherever possible, and tried to get past the smell of poisons that assaulted her senses.

Sarina didn't want to be in the middle of the city any longer than necessary. She hurried over to one of the towering structures and cautiously placed her hand on its carcass. Gripping the building with her fingertips, she climbed the side of the high-rise to get the layout of the city and found a place to her liking forty kilometres south-west.

There the landscape had a more natural appearance and the human dwellings seemed further apart. She felt her hunting instincts kick in, and realised she had picked up on the trace of a predator. Casting out her vampire senses, she discovered the existence of a lone Gatherer further along the coastline. Sarina loosened her hold on the wall and slid to the footpath. She headed off in her chosen direction and reached her suburb of choice within minutes.

Access to her temporary home came to her by chance. An elderly gentleman thought he had glimpsed something in the middle of the street. He swerved, almost losing control of his vehicle. Sarina had seen the headlights and waited in the shadows for it to pass. Once the car had come to a stop and the man had exited the vehicle, Sarina stepped into view, projecting a picture of beauty, as he tried to find the cause of his fright.

Spotting her on the side of the road he said, "I'm sorry, Miss, I nearly didn't see you. Are you okay?"

Sarina used her mind linking abilities so they could understand each other when they talked. "I'm a little bit shaken," she said with a smile, turning up her vampire charm.

He walked towards her as though in a trance. He was completely smitten with her and was willing to do whatever she wanted. 'Fancy a young, beautiful woman like her taking an *interest in me.'* She had long, ebony hair that feathered around the delicate features of her face. The paleness of her skin made the red of her lips seem as deep in colour as a strawberry. Her eyes were dark and mysterious while her chin and cheekbones created a delicate frame.

She tilted his head to the side and pierced his throat with her fangs. Sarina drank just enough blood to take the edge off her thirst and discover everything there was to know about the changes that had occurred to the landscape on Earth. When she had gotten what she needed, she wiped the puncture marks with her tongue, her saliva sealing the wounds, then connected with his mind once more.

"Carl, you are going to get back in your car and go home. I will arrive on your doorstep shortly and you will give me a hug and invite me in. You will tell the friends in your street that your mother is sick and you have to leave to take care of her. I will be house-sitting for you while you are gone. You will tell them you don't know when you will be back. You will not return home until I contact you. Now go quickly and forget this incident completely."

Two

Gemma sat at the desk in her room with her mathematics textbook opened in front of her. She loved numbers and found the work easy. The principal at her school had sent a letter home requesting permission from her parents to place Gemma in the new mathematics extension class that had been formed for year nine. Gemma was excited by the prospect of being part of the new program and wanted to ensure she was able to keep up with the new curriculum demands.

Gaining access to this class would set her up for the rest of her high school years in the fields of maths and science. Unlike most fifteen year olds, Gemma knew what she wanted to do with her life when she left school. She had chosen subjects that would enable her to enter university to study education when she finished school. Most of the kids in her classes hated maths, which was one of the reasons she wanted to become a teacher. Gemma hoped to be able to pass on her love of numbers and make the learning of mathematics more interesting to others.

She believed that everything in life could be explained by mathematical equations; a universal language that everybody had the ability to understand, if it was just explained the right way. It was her brother's struggle with maths that had put her on this career path. Bastian, who was two years older than her, had decided at a young age that maths was way too hard. No matter what his teachers did or said, he would not even try to complete the work they set for him. He would listen to Gemma, though, and sometimes she could help him understand the problem in front of him so that he came up with the correct solution.

Gemma was his lifeline. She didn't make him feel stupid and she explained the concepts in a more simplified manner than his teachers at school. Gemma had the knack of explaining how the differing strands of maths could be applied in everyday life. This gave his curriculum outline some much-needed context and a reason for his brain to try to understand what she was showing him.

Gemma read the next problem in her textbook. Her head tilted to the right as she twisted the light brown hair in her ponytail around the pointer finger of her right hand. Her left pointer finger moved beneath the words as she read them. She raised her feet onto their toes and then lowered them again as her mind contemplated what she was being asked. Usually she sat with her left leg tucked beneath her on the chair while her right foot rested on the floor. As she was still wearing her school uniform, the dark green pencil skirt was too tight to allow her to use her natural posture. Gemma finished reading the question, then picked up her pencil. She was writing the formula for calculating the surface area of a rectangular prism into her notebook, when Bastian knocked on the door.

"Hey, Gemma, I need some help with maths. Can I come in?"

"Sure," she replied with some excitement. Bastian was in year eleven and was studying maths A. While it was not as complicated as maths B or C, it was certainly a lot harder than the work provided in her own textbook. Gemma loved tutoring him. It enabled her to get access to more interesting stuff than she was able to get her hands on at school.

"Thanks, Gem," he said as he opened her door and walked to the spare chair she kept beside her desk for him. The chair belonged to Bastian anyway, but he never sat at his desk to do his homework. He always spread his books across his bed in a very disorderly manner. His desk had clothes, books and CD's dumped all over its surface, making it impossible for him to do any work there. Gemma's desk was immaculate. Her drawers had organiser inserts giving her immediate access to anything she required.

Bastian placed his textbook on her desk. He removed his school jacket, placing it on the back of the chair, then loosened his tie, while Gemma closed her textbook and put it to the side. "What are you working on?" she asked.

"We are learning financial mathematics this term. I have to work out the profit or loss of a company and come up with ways of increasing their profit margin," he stated unhappily.

"It's okay, Bastian. By the time we are finished, you will be able to do this with your eyes closed," she assured him.

"I wish I was as good at maths as you are," he said quietly.

"You get an A+ for English, history, geography and French. It's okay for you to have a subject you struggle with," she reminded him.

"How did you know about that?" he asked with embarrassment.

"Mum and Dad were spruiking about it last week when they received your report card," she told him.

"What did you get on yours?" he asked out of curiosity.

"An A for maths and science, C's and D's for everything else," she said, shrugging her shoulders.

"I can help you with the other subjects, Gem. This tutoring stuff can work both ways, you know."

"Thanks, Bastian," Gemma said with surprise. She helped him more out of love for him than her love for maths although the difference was pretty negligible. She hadn't realized he would be interested in helping his little sister. Bastian was an Olympics contender in gymnastics and she thought he would've been too busy to help her with her school work. He was pretty good looking and there were heaps of girls who wanted to hang off his arm.

Gemma got up to change places with him and found her eyes drawn to the window. The light on Mr. Cameron's porch had just come on. He was an elderly man who seemed to have been forgotten by everybody. Gemma sometimes wondered if the old grump had ever had friends when he was younger. The years had certainly not been kind to him, with thousands of wrinkles and a painful looking stoop to his spine. She couldn't ever remember Mr. Cameron receiving visitors. Night had fallen, so it was unlikely to be canvassers. There appeared to be a woman in old fashioned clothing knocking on his door.

"Check that out," Gemma said to Bastian.

He peeked through the window and wolf whistled. The girl across the road had moved to the side while she waited for Mr. Cameron and by the way her clothing sat, he could tell she had a hot body.

"Hmm, I hope she comes to our door," he said.

"You are so gross," Gemma complained, suddenly losing interest. "What scenario have you been given?" she asked, referring to his textbook.

"Hang on a second," Bastian grumbled.

Gemma realised they were not going to get any work done while the girl stood beneath the light, so she grabbed his textbook off her desk and flopped on her bed. Gemma moved to the contents page and found a chapter on velocity. She wanted to work out how long it would take for them to get from home to the coast on the weekend. Gemma suffered from motion sickness and wanted to know how many motion sickness tablets she would need to stop the queasy feeling she always got when they travelled.

Bastian observed Mr. Cameron open the door and hug the young woman enthusiastically. Mr. Cameron then stepped aside and allowed her entry to his home before closing the door behind them.

"The old man hugged her and let her in," he remarked with surprise.

"Are you sure?" Gemma asked, regaining some interest.

"I just saw it with my own eyes. Fancy that," he said, looking at Gemma lying on her bed with his textbook.

"Maybe she's a relative," Gemma replied, shrugging her shoulders.

"Yeah. That would make sense. I hope she's staying for a while," he stated.

Gemma shook her head. She had never been interested in that lovey-dovey stuff and was pretty sure he was thinking of trying to kiss her.

Bastian looked back out the window and saw Mr. Cameron walking towards their house. He stood up quickly and left Gemma's room. She called after him but he ignored her, racing down the stairs to try to catch the conversation that was about to occur between Mr. Cameron and their parents. Gemma rolled off the bed and peered out the window. She hurried after Bastian, not wanting to be the only one who didn't know what was going on. She reached the top of the staircase as Mr. Cameron rang the doorbell.

Bastian was already there, and opened the door.

Mr. Cameron's shoulders slumped just a little further when he saw Bastian before him. His light brown eyes closed slightly and his smile faltered for a second. His nose and ear hairs were visible and were the same light grey colour as the remaining hair on his head. He was completely bald on top, with a thin spattering of hair from the tip of his ear line to the base of his skull. He had a moustache and facial hair on his chin. His cheeks were clean shaven and the skin, like that of his forehead, was lined like the branches of a Christmas tree. He wore a short-sleeved, beige, button-up shirt with dark brown pants, belt and tan lace-up shoes.

"Good evening, Mr. Cameron," Bastian said.

"Lad. Are your parents home?" Mr. Cameron asked, stopping any hope of conversation between the two.

"Yes, Sir, I'll just get them. Won't you come in?"

"I'll wait here, thank you," Mr. Cameron replied.

"Who's at the door?" their mother, Karen, asked, stepping out of the kitchen, wiping her hands on her apron. Her curious, blue eyes looked at Bastian as she waited for an answer.

"Mr. Cameron, from across the street," Bastian replied as he walked to the bottom step to sit with Gemma who had moved closer to the action.

"Run along, you two," Karen encouraged as she walked towards the door. She removed the apron, revealing a simple but stylish sleeveless dress in midnight blue. She placed the apron on a coat hook located near the front door and said, "Hello, Carl, is everything all right?"

Gemma and Bastian looked at one another. They didn't know their mother was on first name terms with the cranky old man across the street. Karen and Walter, her husband, often played cards with Carl at his place on a Friday night after Gemma had gone to bed. They thought Bastian was at home to look after her if anything happened. Little did they know he often snuck out to meet his girlfriend, Sarah, at the park up the road.

"Hello, Karen. I'm afraid not. My mother has taken ill and I need to take care of her for a while. I am not sure how long I will be gone. My niece, Sarina, has come to look after Max while I am gone. She is a nurse and works the night shift so you probably won't see much of her. Sarina has assured me she is capable of feeding him in the morning, and taking him for walks in the evening before she begins work."

"I'm sorry to hear about your mother. I hope she recovers quickly," Karen said.

"Thank you for your kind thoughts, Karen, but she probably won't pull through this time. I best be off."

"It doesn't sound like Max is happy to have her there. Are you sure you wouldn't rather we take care of him? The back is fully fenced and the kids would love to spend some time with him," Karen said, as Max's continued growls began to escalate in volume.

"Hmmm, maybe that might be a good idea. Sarina can keep an eye on the house and you can keep an eye on Max. I'll bring him over, if that's okay?"

"Sure it is, Carl. Anything you need. Bastian can go home with you and give you a hand gathering his stuff." Karen assured him.

"Yes," Bastian said enthusiastically, causing Gemma to roll her eyes.

Carl didn't want to offend Karen by declining. She had been a good neighbour, but he had often seen Bastian exiting the house on a Friday night, leaving Gemma unattended. Carl had also seen him climb out the window and take off up the street to meet with his girl on a number of other occasions. He believed the boy to be a regular healthy teenager and as such, wanted him nowhere near his niece.

"Don't you be thinking of coming over here all the time when I am gone, Lad. Sarina has responsibilities and doesn't have time to pander to the whims of a smitten boy."

"No, Sir. I am quite busy myself with the Olympics only a few months away," Bastian replied undeterred. He was sure Sarina could make up her own mind of what she had time for, and he was sure she would make some for him, once she saw him.

Three

Mr. Cameron hurried home, believing it was imperative he was at his mother's side as quickly as possible.

Bastian was right behind him, eager to introduce himself to the new girl on the block. Thoughts of Sarah were pushed far into the recesses of his mind. Perhaps that would change when he saw this woman face to face. Just because her body was an attractive shape from across the street, silhouetted by the light on the veranda, it didn't mean that her face was pleasant to look upon.

Mr. Cameron threw open the door and called to Sarina, who was on the other side of the house. She was organising better protective measures for the doors and windows to protect herself from the coming sunlight. She was by his side in seconds, eager to meet the new smell he had brought home with him.

"Sarina, this is Bastian. He lives across the street and won't cause you any problems. He is just here to pick up Max so you don't have to worry about him while I am gone."

"You didn't need to organise that, Uncle Carl. It is no trouble at all for me to take care of the Rottweiler while you are gone," she responded.

"Is that why he is growling at you?" Bastian remarked.

Sarina glared at him. This one had a mouth on him and thought he was pretty good with the ladies. She contemplated the thought of eating him herself, but AB positive blood was very hard to come by and was the sweetest of them all. Sarina found it necessary to inject her meals with blood thinners whenever she indulged herself with this delicacy. The blood tended to coagulate very quickly and once the blood became lumpy, she found it hard to swallow.

His blood, however, would make a very nice present for her new mate, when she turned him. She decided to play the part of a demure, uncertain woman. That should keep a guy that was young, fit and confident in his abilities to attract the opposite sex, persistent in his endeavours to spend some time with her. How nice it was to have a sacrifice arrive on her doorstep, eager to please.

While Carl gathered Max's things together, Sarina engaged Bastian in conversation.

"Are you off to somewhere important?" she began.

"I beg your pardon?" Bastian asked not understanding the question.

Sarina pointed to his outfit, "You are very nicely dressed for eating dinner at home."

"What, this?" At her nod, he continued, "I had a meeting with the Olympic committee this afternoon after school and have only just gotten home. This is my school uniform. I haven't had a chance to get changed yet." he explained.

"The Olympics," Sarina nodded having no idea what that was. "Must be pretty good then?"

"Yes, I am. Even if I do say so myself."

"Hi, I'm Sarina," she said holding out her hand. Bastian took it in his and gave a strong handshake. As she let go, she scratched his palm with her claw and brought a few drops of blood to the surface. She dragged her pointer finger through and turned her body away from him, placing the finger in her mouth. She managed to see flashes of Bastian in his singlet and shorts doing all sorts of gymnastic feats on the horse, rings, bars and floor. He had a nice physique and was very strong. His blood was filled with lots of beneficial vitamins and minerals that her new partner would require to begin his new life as a vampire.

"I guess you have a lot of girls vying for your attention," she said as she turned to face him once more and ran her finger from his shoulder to his elbow.

Bastian's chest puffed out instantly and his spine straightened in response to her remark. Sarina came to the quick realisation that, while humans had become more industrious in her absence, that was pretty much the extent of their evolutionary process. Males still fell instantly under her spell, believing in the projection of a beautiful, seductive woman standing before them. She wondered if the females still had the ability to see her as she truly was, absolutely frightful with bluish-grey skin; sharp pointy teeth; red, hungry eyes; blackened claws for fingernails, and the smell of death that clung to her like a revoltingly, overpowering perfume.

Bastian grabbed her hand. "There is no ring on your finger. Does this mean that you are not currently in a serious relationship?"

"I am currently between relationships," she confirmed as she untangled herself from his grip.

He moved in closer to her and wrapped his arm around her waist pulling her close. "Would you like to have dinner with me tonight?"

"Won't that upset your mother's plans?" she replied with her own question.

Damn, he hadn't thought of that. Karen would have his dinner ready in half an hour and would be annoyed if he didn't stay and eat it. "Would you like to come over and eat with us? I am sure cooking dinner is the last thing you want to do and Mum always cooks more than we need. It will be delicious."

"Thank you for the offer, Bastian," she said, looking deep into his hazel eyes, "but I already have plans for dinner."

"Do you have a date?" he asked as his eyes lowered to her lips and his head began to move closer to hers.

"No, just plans," she answered in a whisper.

"Hey kid, can you give me a hand," Carl called from the basement.

"He's talking to you," Sarina stated.

"Hmmm," he murmured.

"You better go before he comes up and sees you manhandling me," she suggested, turning her head to the side.

"Mr. Cameron?"

"Down here, son. I can't quite pick up his bed without everything falling off. Can you give me a hand?"

"Sure," Bastian replied. He let Sarina go and walked down the stairs. He grabbed one end of Max's bed while Mr. Cameron grabbed the other. He was a very spoilt dog. His bed was a metre long by half a metre wide and had a scratchy hessian base. On top of that, Mr. Cameron had placed a plush, soft mattress of duck down with a one hundred percent cotton cover. There were also a few boomerang shaped pillows laid there for Max's comfort.

"Sir, your dog is treated better than most of my friends at school."

"Son, my dog treats me better than most of your friends at school treat their loved ones."

Bastian could only nod his head. There was no point in arguing with Mr. Cameron. Bastian wouldn't be able to change his mind, and he would be leaving soon anyway. Arguing would only prolong his departure time.

They carried the bed carefully up the stairs, through the kitchen and out into the foyer where Sarina was waiting with the doors opened. "Be back soon, Love, for the dog and the food," Carl told her.

Sarina nodded her head and walked back into the lounge room. Very soon, she would have the place to herself. She sniffed the air and found another male on her doorstep. This was turning out to be a nightmare. She had needed a place where she could bunker down, stir up some trouble thereby getting the attention of the

Gatherers, who would place her in contact with her new mate. She had not expected the men in the neighbourhood to be clamouring to meet her.

"Hello," Walter called.

"Good evening," Sarina said, stepping into view. The man before her was an older version of his son. He too, had the appearance of an athlete. Where Bastian's hairstyle was short back and sides, this man's hair was longer in the front and flicked to the left hand side.

"My name is Walter. I am Bastian's Dad. Karen, my wife, asked me to come over to invite you for dinner if you haven't already eaten," he said a little breathlessly.

"Well, that is very nice of her, Walter, but as I just explained to Bastian, I already have plans for this evening. Perhaps we can get together another time."

"Hmmm. That sounds great. I will let Karen know. Do you think I could take Max and his food home with me? Carl thought I could help speed up the process so he could be on his way."

"Of course," Sarina replied grabbing the lead from the hook on the wall and handing it to him.

Walter walked out the back, hooked the lead to Max's collar and brought him inside. He growled menacingly at Sarina who smirked in return. She handed Walter the shopping bags containing the cans of wet food and the bag of dry. He said he would ask Karen to get in touch to organise the details of their get together, before walking out the door.

This would work out much better. With the family across the road taking care of Max, she would not need to kill him. If she remembered to contact Carl and let him know he could return, it would be nice for Max to be here to meet him, considering the man's age. Now that the dog was gone, she just had to wait for Carl to begin his journey to his mother's place. Then she would be free to hunt for food and stir up some mayhem for the Gatherers.

It was only a few minutes before Carl returned, with Bastian. Sarina looked at him in bewilderment. What was going on? She hadn't even turned her charms on for him, neither had she taken a bite. Why was he so smitten with her? She had felt the waves of desire pulsing off his Dad, who had managed to control himself and leave with the dog without being prompted. So what was wrong with the son?

"Bastian, what brings you back?" she queried.

"I thought I could help Mr. Cameron pack his bags."

"He is all ready to go, he doesn't need your help," she assured him.

Carl grabbed his keys from the sideboard and kissed Sarina on the cheek. "Take care of yourself, Love, and don't let this one cause you any trouble."

"Goodbye, Uncle, and don't worry. I can take care of myself just fine," she replied.

"I'm sure you can," he said looking deep into her eyes and seeing his own reflection in her pupils. For just a moment, he thought her eyes were red, but when he concentrated harder, his mind became muddled and he pictured dark brown eyes instead.

He walked down the stairs to the basement and went through the connecting door to the garage. Bastian and Sarina heard the grinding gears of the roller-door as it opened, then the sound of the car engine as it spluttered to life. Carl drove slowly through the opening and pressed the button to close it again. Sarina waved goodbye from the porch and then walked back inside with Bastian. She needed to get rid of him, she was hungry and if she didn't go soon, she would not be able to resist drinking his blood.

"Uncle said this was a lovely neighbourhood and that I'd be safe here. He is gone, you can go home now."

"He was right. This is a safe neighbourhood. I would love to show you around," he said.

"You would?" she replied. It would be prudent to have a personal guide of the area so that she could become accustomed to the changes that had occurred in her absence. "Like I said earlier, I have some appointments I have to attend to, but I am free after that. I don't start work until tomorrow night, so until sunrise, I am free to explore the city."

"Sweet. I don't have any training in the morning, so I could stay up a couple of hours later tonight and still get the same amount of sleep before school. Do you drive? I am still on my Learners Permit."

"No, I don't drive," Sarina said.

"We'll just leg it then. Will you be finished by ten?"

"Yes, that should be fine," she agreed.

"Until then."

Sarina watched him cross the road with hungry eyes. She would need to consume quite a few humans to be able to spend time in his company beneath the night's sky. She made her way back to the bedroom and went through the wardrobe in Carl's room. It still held a range of stylish clothes that belonged to his wife when she had been alive. By the looks of the outfits, she used to wear them in her younger days. Sarina preferred black and pulled out the first item of that colour she found. She tried it on and found it to be an off-the-shoulder, mid-thigh length dress that barely covered anything.

She would be able to run perfectly in this outfit and it would excite her male victims when she found them. If Sarina came across a female meal, there would be plenty of skin for her prey to look at and freak out over before she perished. It would add a little bit of spice to the meal and make it more interesting.

Sarina took off her high-heeled boots and viewed the selection of shoes in the case. None of them looked good enough to stand up to the speed with which she ran and would most likely perish. Sarina decided to stay in bare feet. Any injuries she sustained would soon be healed when she fed. Sarina made her way to the front door and closed it gently behind her.

Bastian's scent had increased Sarina's longing to hunt. She had almost forgotten what it was like to be able to choose her own food. There were herds of humans on Mystique that had been provided to feed her and her children. Unfortunately for the vampires, the humans were in poor health with most of them being addicted to drugs. This tainted the taste of the blood but kept the vampires sustained.

The humans here, smelled clean and fresh. She could drain as many of them as she liked without worrying if there would be enough for the next night's meal. Thinking about the thrill of the hunt and the freshness of the prey had made her ravenous. Sarina couldn't wait to get started. She was finally able to hunt and feast.

Four

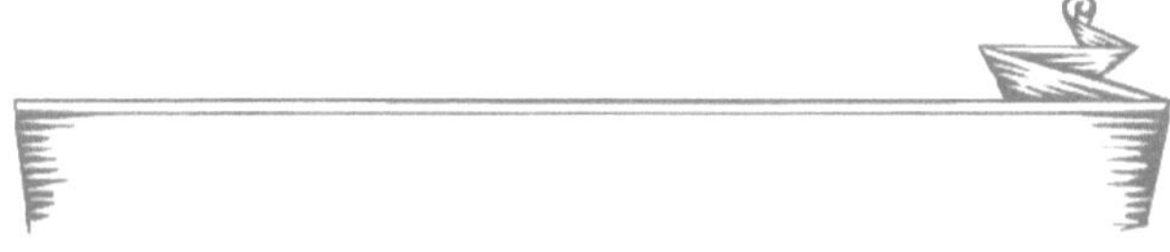
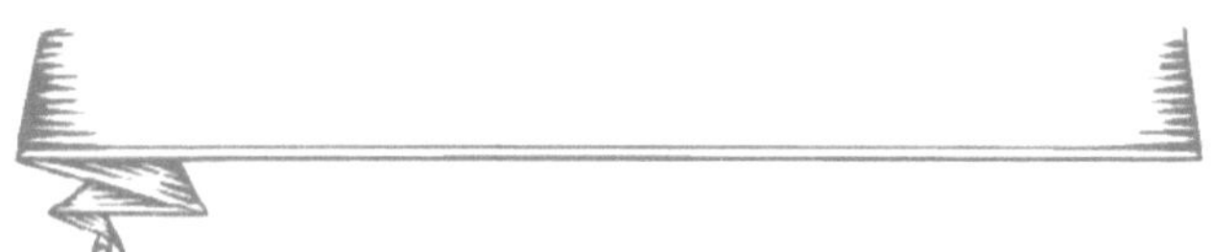

Sarina didn't notice the coolness of the air as it caressed her skin. She was focussed on feeding her hunger and drawing the attention of the Gatherers who were currently protecting the area from creatures such as herself.

She ran, fast. The wind whipped her hair about her face as she sprinted towards the national forest where a Locator Fairy was eating.

Sarina made sure her mind was open to inspection and thought of the most gruesome things to draw attention to her position. Sarina sensed the fairy listening intently to the universe as she detected trouble on her radar. Then their minds collided in a very powerful moment.

Sarina felt the purity of the good magic that existed within the creature she was seeking, and the fairy felt the pure vileness of her. The game had begun and she was determined to win.

She perceived the fairy's alarm and through their connection, felt the pulse of energy the fairy sent out to summon the nearest Gatherer for assistance. Unfortunately, the answering warrior was female. While this was not devastating to Sarina's plans, it certainly would not be as easy as she had hoped. The female would most likely not be susceptible to her charms and would come at her with full force.

Sarina was not concerned for her safety, being more powerful than the Gatherers, but they had something she needed; the Gatherer that had captured her and her mate Karayan, all those years ago. She had been attracted to him then, but thought that her life with Karayan would be eternal. Now that his life had been ended by a Battle Star, it was time to make her captor a captive of hers, for eternity.

Sarina had planned on skirting only the edges of the forest to make contact with the Locator. She was delightfully surprised to discover a couple out for a walk, who had her favourite blood, Type O. She loved the savoury taste and the smooth texture of the liquid. Type O blood took longer to coagulate than the others and she was able to finish her meal before it became lumpy. Fortunately, humans with this blood type made up approximately fifty percent of the Earth's population.

She really wanted to play with her food but was too hungry. The taste of Carl earlier had given her an indication of what healthier tasting blood would be like, and having resisted the scent of Bastian, she could no longer wait. Sarina was approaching the couple from behind and chose to pounce on the male first. He would taste yummy; but the female would be scrumptious, once she saw that her mate had been murdered and she got a good look at the creature that had killed him.

"What are you doing?" the woman giggled as her boyfriend lurched forward, nearly taking her with him.

Her giggles soon turned to shrieks as she noticed Sarina perched on his back. "Get off him, Freak!" the woman yelled as she tried to drag Sarina off.

Sarina stood up and wiped her face with the back of her hand. She lifted the woman up by her chin and carried her so they were standing beneath a light along the path. The woman's shrieks of anger quickly turned to fear, as she was carted around like a bag of lollies, and saw Sarina for what she was.

"That's it, scream as loudly as you can. The more humans the merrier," Sarina laughed. The woman seemed to be going into shock. It made no difference to Sarina's enjoyment. It wouldn't negatively affect the flow of blood through her veins in the time it took Sarina to drink it.

The woman kicked and scratched, all minor irritations. All of the injuries the woman inflicted upon Sarina healed instantaneously. Sarina toyed with the idea of letting the woman go and chasing her but decided against it. There wasn't any fun in that sort of hunting, so she sank her fangs into the woman's neck and drank deeply. Once she had been drained, Sarina let her body fall, to move on to more exciting quarry.

Now that her hunger had been quenched, it was time to become reacquainted with her skills as a predator. They had not been required during her imprisonment on Mystique, and she felt rather rusty. Sarina decided she would not stand for the current circumstances surrounding their nutritional requirements for much longer. Once her new mate was by her side, she would have access to insider information that would enable her to accomplish many things, including the release of her people.

Sarina ran south. It wasn't time to hit the more populated areas of the country. She wanted to find her Gatherer, not spend her time eluding the ones protecting the coastline. After running for twenty minutes, she came across a young woman who seemed quite upset. There wouldn't be much hunting involved in securing this meal so she kept going. Sarina longed for action and she found it, five kilometres further down the road.

A group of men were running around in a clearing. They wore white polo shirts with red trim; short, red shorts; white socks with red stripes; and white joggers. They were strong, sweaty and she matched her advancement to the rhythm of their heartbeats as their blood surged through their veins.

Sarina ran into the middle of the pack and grabbed a tall, stocky fellow around the waist. He should have melted as their eyes locked together but Sarina took steps to ensure he saw her for what she was. She watched as his head narrowly missed being hit by the football as she moved his neck to provide herself with better access.

The other men watched on jealously, having no idea where she had come from. They shouted encouraging words to their mate as the woman placed her mouth on his throat. Their voices almost drowned out his screams of pain as she drank from him.

"Hey, what's going on?" the closest guy said, moving in even closer.

"Your friend is dead. Who is next?" Sarina questioned as she allowed them all to see who she really was. Her laughter rang out as she jogged to the other side of the field. The men checked on their friend and discovered he actually was dead.

"What was that thing?" questioned one of the men.

"I don't know, but I am going to kill it," the closest guy said to his teammates before taking off after her.

All of the men except two were right behind her. They ran as fast as they could but had nothing on her. She kept just far enough ahead so they could see where she had gone, before doubling back and feeding on the two men who had been too scared to follow.

Sarina had lured the men into a wooded area. It wasn't very large, only a square kilometre. The men split up in an attempt to box her in. Sarina returned to the area and began the hunt.

She stalked the men one by one, revelling in the freedom to live as she was born to, on her awakening. Sarina did not remember being human, too many years had passed. She did remember a time when her kind wandered the Earth, hunting, feeding and loving on their own terms. Sarina hated her imprisonment and cursed the ones who had made it so.

She moved faster than their eyes could see. The men could sense her presence instinctively but could not catch sight of her. They spun on the spot, searching for her without success. As she moved, their fear levels rose. They called to one another, but none of them had found the creature that had murdered their friend.

Sarina continued to play with them. She would come across one of the men and pause long enough for him to see her and call to his friends before disappearing and turning up in front of another. She felt their feelings of fear turn into feelings of frustration. That was good. She was amazed at how little humans had changed since she had been on Earth. They had not developed any protective devices that she could see and didn't seem to know how important it was to do so.

Keeping the humans safe, in Sarina's opinion, had been a very bad idea for their evolutionary process. She stood before a male who held some sort of object in his hand. He yelled, "Eat this!" as he pulled the trigger. Sarina felt a sharp pain in the middle of her forehead and placed her fingers on the spot of entry. She was surprised to see her blood on their tips as she pulled them away from her face.

Her body pushed the bullet out of her head through its entry point, where it fell and landed at her feet. Sarina bent down and picked it up, turning it over in her hand. She sorted through her newly acquired memories for details on the object and discovered that man had found a way to protect himself after all. Pity it could never hurt her kind or many of the other creatures that were housed on Mystique.

By this time, her body had healed itself and the man stood before her, frozen with shock and fear. "Good try," Sarina told him as she approached, slowly.

"You should be dead," he kept repeating, as he watched her advance.

Sarina was impressed with this one's courage and decided to make his death easier for him. He was the first to take a stand against her and she allowed him the luxury of being intoxicated by her powers. His eyes saw her as the beautiful seductress she projected and his feet propelled him forward to meet her.

Her hand ran through his short auburn hair. She captured his green eyes with her own and took him by the hand. Turning his palm up, she lifted his arm so his wrist rested on her lips.

Sarina bit hard, piercing his artery and allowing the hot, rich fluid to flow down her throat. Instead of shrieks of pain, there were moans of ecstasy.

Two of his friends came upon them from different directions, having heard him fire his weapon. They watched in horror as they saw their mate, a policeman, being drained of his life force, but seeming to enjoy it. The captain of the group burst through the trees. He took in the scene before him and lowered his eyes. He saw Tom's gun lying on the ground, picked it up, checked the safety was off and fired the remaining five bullets into her back.

Her body jerked as each bullet hit but didn't stop her from feeding. The men were amazed that she still stood. If bullets didn't take her down, they had no idea what would, but knew that they couldn't stand idle while their friend was in trouble. As though they could read each other's mind, they ran at her simultaneously. They tried to knock her over and when that didn't work, pull her off their friend. They were unable to get her to loosen her grip on her meal. When she was finished with her meal, she simply grabbed the next one and began feeding from him.

The other two realised they were no match for her and took off for their cars. The slowest only got halfway before she caught up to him. The fastest reached his door but was yanked back before he could open it.

Sarina was glowing with excitement. Her hunger and lust for hunting had been satiated for the time being, and she decided to head back to Carl's place. She had no idea what the time was but felt confident enough to be able to walk into the darkness with Bastian without incident.

Sarina hoped she would have time to change her outfit before Bastian spotted her. She was pretty sure there were holes in her dress at the back where the bullets had penetrated her body. Although her body was able to heal, she was pretty sure that human clothes would not be able to do so. They were a lot less advanced than their Gatherer cousins who had outfits that could transform and repair themselves.

Sarina didn't come across any more humans on her journey home. She was disappointed to not have connected with the Gatherer yet. Surely they were usually quicker to respond to a threat to humans than this. Perhaps there weren't as many of them on Earth as there were on Mystique. She had not thought to gather this information from Adair before she left. The only thing that had been on her mind was finding the one that was to be her new mate and getting home to her children.

Sarina enjoyed running across the landscape that was so different to what she was used to. The textures beneath her feet were unlike anything she was exposed to on Mystique and she realised, once again, how oppressive her life had become. She knew the Locator Fairy had zeroed in on her location and was following her route. Once she had gotten within ten kilometres of Carl's place, she closed her mind to inspection. Sarina wanted them to know the vicinity of her whereabouts without being able to pinpoint the exact position of her residence.

Sarina arrived home and raced to the bedroom to change her outfit. She needed something attractive without being too revealing. Bastian was already smitten with her. She looked in the wardrobe and found a floor length dress in black and white stripes. It didn't have sleeves but did have wide straps and was high cut along the chest area.

Sarina removed her outfit and threw it in the rubbish bin. No point in keeping that one now that it had bullet holes in it. She donned the new dress and looked for shoes. She found some pretty high-heeled black and white shoes on the floor of the wardrobe and found them to also be in her size.

Sarina had begun her walk towards the lounge room when the doorbell rang. She sniffed the air and discovered that Bastian had arrived. Sarina put a smile on her face and wandered to the front door. She opened it and noticed that Bastian had changed too.

VAMPIRE

He was wearing a pair of tight blue jeans, long-sleeved purple t-shirt and brown loafers. He looked happy and expectant and Sarina realised that she was loathe to spend time with Bastian this evening, even though she knew what a special gift he would be to her new love. She had enjoyed herself so much earlier, she realised she wanted to experience as much hunting freedom as possible before returning to Mystique.

Sarina decided to invite him in, make him believe that they had spent some time together and then send him home again. She closed the door behind him so any nosy neighbours wouldn't be able to see what she was doing. She placed her hands on his chest and pushed until he rested against the back of the front door. Then she bit him on the neck taking a small amount of blood and discovered everything he had learnt in the short time he had been alive.

Sarina was surprised to discover the technological advances the humans had made in communication devices. She filed that bit of information at the forefront of her mind for easy access should she require it in the near future. She sent him home after instructing him that they had been on an hour's walk around town. He had done a fine job of showing her where to find food and where to locate other places of interest while she was in town. Bastian went home to get ready for bed.

Gemma, who was supposed to have already fallen asleep, had been sitting at her desk trying to complete her English homework. She had left it until last because she found it so difficult but then couldn't sleep, because she didn't know what to do and hadn't gotten it finished. She had seen Bastian leave their house and make his way across the road, only to return a few minutes later.

She walked to the top of the stairs to ask him for help with her homework. He looked at her blankly as he climbed the staircase. When she asked if he was okay, he ignored her and continued to his room. Gemma noticed the two puncture marks on his neck and came to the conclusion they had a vampire living across the street. She decided she would need to keep an eye on her brother and do some research on the internet for ways to protect him from Sarina.

Five

Thanks to Bastian, Sarina had discovered how to use a watch to tell the time. She grabbed Carl's spare watch off the nightstand and placed it on her arm to ensure she would be home before sunrise. Time to have some more fun, and grab the attention of the Gatherer who would lead her new mate to her location.

VAMPIRE

Sarina waited until she saw the last of the lights turn off across the road before leaving the house again. She ran in the other direction, this time giving the Gatherer a chance to pinpoint her starting position within a twenty-kilometre area.

Once she had reached the ten-kilometre mark, Sarina opened her mind once more to inspection and brought up the memories of her earlier hunting expedition. She felt her excitement rise as she remembered the experience and used her keen sense of smell to locate the next region of human activity.

A group of people were at a gathering a couple of kilometres ahead. She could smell quite a few adults with a greater number of children in attendance. Sarina's enthusiasm went up another notch as she thought of the fear that would be prevalent within the group once she arrived.

The adults would be terrified for the safety of the children and want to protect them. The children would be scared stiff when they realised their nightmares had come to life. Sarina had already decided before she arrived that this would be a night to remember for many years to come.

There were seven adults sitting in the rotunda in the park with another two at the barbeques cooking marshmallows. The children were climbing all over the swings, monkey bars and slippery slides under the glow of the safety lights, not that they would be of any help.

Sarina crept over to the oldest child, who was sitting forlornly on the seesaw waiting for somebody to come and join him. She leaned on the seat up in the air so that she could mount it and watched as a smile spread across the young boy's face.

"Thanks for playing with me," the boy said.

Sarina didn't reply as they went up and down on the seesaw.

"Are you here with someone?" he asked.

Sarina shook her head and kept quiet.

"Who are you?" he questioned.

"You're worst nightmare," Sarina stated as she moved to his end of the seesaw in an instant, placed her hands around his throat and lifted him high in the air. He tried to scream, but couldn't. Neither could he suck any air into his lungs. Sarina laughed as his face went from pink, to rose, to red, to purple. His eyes began to bulge in their sockets as though they were going to pop out of his head. Sarina flung him twenty metres through the air where he landed on the lap of one of the women in the rotunda.

"What the hell?" she screamed in fright mingled with pain, as her shoulder blades slammed into the table situated behind her, and her legs were driven into the hard, wooden seat by the weight of the boy.

He rolled off her lap to land painfully on the cement floor. He was dry retching as he desperately tried to get air into his lungs. The women sprang to their feet and the men had raced out into the playground in response to their instincts to protect their loved ones from danger.

The other children had not noticed their family member sailing through the air like a superhero. They were too busy having fun to notice the danger lurking in the shadows until she appeared before them. The girls screamed in a pitch that sent shivers down the spines of all in attendance. It was as grating as the sound of fingernails being dragged across a blackboard.

The adults, temporarily frozen with fear, stared uncomprehendingly in the direction of the children. Sarina enjoyed being able to move faster than the human eye could see. The adults had no idea what the children were screaming about as she had not yet given them an opportunity to see her.

They knew instinctively that something was terribly wrong. Children didn't scream like that without reason and none of them seemed to be hurt, other than the boy who had suddenly flown through the air.

"Toby, what happened?" asked the woman he landed on.

"I was waiting for someone to play with me when this lady sat on the other side of the seesaw. We had a ride together and then she had me around my throat and threw me over here," he cried, as tears and snot ran down his face.

"Toby Harrold Mortimer, what have I told you about lying? Oh for goodness sake, wipe your face," his mother admonished.

"I'm not lying!" he screamed, wiping his face with his forearm. "She picked me up and threw me. Can you please take me home, Mum? I don't feel very well."

His mother took a closer look at him and saw a dark bruise already appearing around his neck. "Oh, Toby," she cried and began packing up. "Sorry, Tam, we are going to have to go. He needs to go to the hospital to have that looked at."

"Yes, I agree," Tammy replied.

"But I want him to stay and play with me," Sarina pouted, placing herself in front of them.

Toby's mum fainted on the spot, hitting her head hard enough on the concrete to make it bleed profusely. Sarina's hand wrapped itself around Tammy's neck but soon let go as she smelled the blood. She had already fed earlier in the night and it shouldn't have had any effect on her, but it did. Her hand let go of Tammy and grabbed Toby's mum instead, lifting her off the ground.

The woman's head lolled to the side and her eyes had rolled in their sockets so only the whites showed. Sarina licked the wound and shuddered with pleasure. She sank her teeth into the woman's throat and savoured the fluid. The flavour was exquisite, like nothing she had ever tasted before.

There was something different about this woman's DNA that made her taste so good, but Sarina didn't know what. She savoured every drop of the delicious, life-giving liquid then searched for more. Toby and two of the other children were obviously spawned from this one and she bled them dry as well.

VAMPIRE

The other adults and children were of no interest to her other than to attract the attention of the Gatherer. One by one, she nicked the arteries in their necks with her claws. Once they had bled out, she left their bodies to litter the parkland.

Sarina decided to keep the second oldest child, a boy of about thirteen years of age, alive until the Gatherer arrived. She used her vampire charms to make him sit quietly on the seat until she had a use for him. Sarina looked at the watch and noticed it had only taken twenty minutes from when she had arrived to when she had finished with the humans.

She hoped the Gatherer wouldn't keep her waiting too long. Sarina was eager to begin the next chapter of her life with her new mate. She knew the Locator Fairy had picked her up on that special radar thing they had. This time, Sarina would wait for the Gatherer, but make it look as though she was interrupting Sarina's hunt.

April, the Gatherer, didn't keep her waiting too long. She had already been alerted to Sarina's presence earlier in the night and had left immediately. As Sarina had decided to travel in the other direction for the second hunt, it had actually brought her closer to where April had originated from, allowing their paths to intersect.

Sarina had picked her up from thirty kilometres away and was surprised at the speed with which she travelled. Everything became clear when the car April was driving came to a screeching halt a few metres from where Sarina waited impatiently. She had told the boy to stand before her until April had closed the distance, then to scream as though his life depended on it. He was very good at following instructions and April fell for the scenario presented to her.

"Let the boy go, vampire," April asserted.

"Or what? I have it on good authority that you aren't allowed to kill me," Sarina replied.

"Whose authority would that be?" April questioned.

"Adair, your Queen."

April was momentarily speechless. She couldn't fathom how this creature would know about her Queen and the directive to not kill the creatures under any circumstances.

"I can see you are a little flustered . . ." Sarina began before being cut off.

"Vampire, you do not belong here. You will be relocated to the planet, Mystique, where your every need will be taken care of. An escort will arrive shortly. I have no qualms at all in causing great suffering to you should the need arise," April stated matter-of-factly.

Sarina quite liked this Gatherer. She didn't cower before her and was not overly confident in her ability to handle the situation which probably meant she was quite proficient at her job. Her long, blonde hair with caramel highlights had been braided. Sarina assumed this was more for personal safety than for fashion. She wore a royal blue coloured shirt with a paisley panel across the chest. She had dark blue pants that disappeared into flat, knee-high boots in the same colour. Her dark blue eyes blazed with confidence.

"I'll tell you what," Sarina said amicably, "you get on that communication device of yours and ask your superiors for my current location, Queen Sarina, ruler of the Land of Darkness. Then you tell them to locate the Gatherer named Toranthian and send him to this location. They have forty-five hours, to get organised. If he is not here when I return, there will be a thousand deaths before the sun rises. You can have this male as a gesture of good will. I only want the Gatherer who imprisoned me three thousand years ago."

Sarina was gone. April blinked in surprise. She had forgotten how fast they moved and realised how unprepared she had been. She had forgotten to get the silver net from the boot of the car in her haste to protect the boy. There was nothing she wanted more than to go after her, but there were bodies that needed to be taken care of.

April pulled out her phone and called the number for the Starlight Investigations Communication Centre. "Hi, Sophia, it's April."

"Hi, April, how's it going? Need a Collector?"

"Yeah, I am going to need one. Sophia, I've got a situation, can you ping my phone and get the GPS coordinates of my location."

"Got you. What do you need?"

"I've got probably two dozen bodies, strewn across a public park area that needs to be taken care of before dawn."

"What, at this hour?" Sophia gasped.

"It gets worse, most of them are children."

"What are they doing having children out at this time of night and on a school night?" Sophia questioned.

"Your guess is as good as mine," April answered.

"What creature are you hunting?"

"A vampire, who claims to be Queen Sarina from the Land of Darkness. Can you check with the security detail on Mystique to find out what you can about this Queen Sarina? This vamp, who claims to be her, is requesting a reunion with Toranthian. Can you see if he was the one who originally captured her? She has given us forty-five hours to have him here. She has promised to not kill any more humans until then. If the Gatherer is our Toren, I would like to know how he got her the first time if, on the off chance, she has escaped Mystique and made her way back here."

"April, you know it is not possible to escape Mystique with all the protective measures that have been put in place there."

"Yeah I know, Sophia," she said, rubbing her eyes in an attempt to prevent the tears that threatened to fall. "Can you just ask around?"

"Of course, April. We are here to provide whatever support you need."

"Oh, and Sophia, there is another site that needs attention. I will call again when I get there so you will have the exact coordinates for the clean-up team. Can you let the others know to expect my call and be on standby?"

"Sure, April. You are doing a great job, you know."

"Yeah, I know. Thanks, Sophia."

"Talk to you soon, and April, take care of yourself. Vampires are among the most dangerous creatures you guys have to deal with. Maybe you should get some help with this one. Force took on one a few years ago and nearly became one of the suckers himself. Sorry, pun not intended."

"I'll keep that in mind," April said with a chuckle. She loved talking to Sophia who always managed to make her laugh.

April pulled the map out of the glove box and placed a dot to mark their current position. She placed the map in the compartment and then waited impatiently for the clean-up crew to materialise.

It would take her over an hour to drive to the other place and she worried that somebody would stumble across the site before she could get there. Once the clean-up crew arrived, she showed them the damage the vampire had done and they discussed the story that would be given to the police department regarding the deaths of their citizens. Weary from the emotional effect of the scene and her constant wonderings about what she would find at the next one, she headed back to the car and opened the door. She was pleased to see that her Locator Fairy had caught up to her and was waiting in the car.

Briella's natural look was like that of all fairies. Lilac coloured hair and irises, and wings that were blue and purple, patterned like a peacock's tail. With April's help, her hair had been coloured with food colouring to be an almost fluorescent lime green. They had also been experimenting with food colouring to change the colour of her wings which were currently a lime green with darker coloured splotches. The emerald coloured contact lenses that April had successfully shrunk to fit Briella's tiny eyes could not hide the feeling of concern that emanated from her miniature friend.

Briella's new look was fashioned to match her outfit which consisted of long, lime green harem pants with aqua waist band and a lime green shirt which was fastened together with a button in the middle of her breasts. Her feet, which swung backwards and forwards as she perched on top of the steering wheel, were covered with off-white, slip-on shoes. She had retrieved her headset in anticipation of April's return. As soon as the radio spluttered to life, Briella began to speak. April adjusted the volume until Briella's voice was clearly audible.

"Are you all right, April?"

"Yes, Briella, I'm fine. How do I get to the first slaughter site?"

Briella gave directions while April drove in silence. There were a lot of negative thoughts flying around April's head that she wanted to keep to herself. At least the vampire was female and wouldn't be able to coerce her into doing her bidding. Sophia was right, it would probably be better if she were able to team up with one of the other Gatherers in the area. April felt however, it would be safer to find an available female Gatherer to help her with this vampire, than to call on one of her male Gatherer friends.

April pushed the button for the hands-free and soon had Sophia on the line. "Hey, Sophia, can you tell me if Layla or Rochelle is on a case at present?"

April heard the tapping of keys through the phone before Sophia replied. "Layla is currently hunting a poltergeist and Rochelle is pursuing a phantasm."

"Whoa, both originating from the ghostly plane. Okay, thanks Sophia."

"Do you want me to let you know when they have completed their tasks?" Sophia questioned.

"No, it's okay. I've got this. If you could let me know as soon as you have any information on Queen Sarina and contacted Toranthian that would be more than enough help."

"I'm on it, my sweet."

VAMPIRE

April and Briella arrived at the site where Sarina's other victims lay. She called Starlight Investigations which was answered by a different team member, Samuel.

"Good evening. Starlight Investigations. Samuel speaking."

"Hi, Samuel, it's April. I need a clean-up crew at this location. Do you have my GPS coordinates?"

"Yes, April, I have them. Do you require anything else this evening?"

"No thanks."

"Thank you for your call, April. Please call again if you require further assistance."

"I swear Samuel is a computer and not a real guy," April said to Briella as she hung up the phone.

"Why do you say that?" asked Briella.

"Never mind." She wasn't in the mood to impersonate him for Briella's benefit. "Do you mind if I have a nap while waiting for the clean-up crew to arrive?"

"No, go right ahead," Briella answered. "I might fly up to that light pole and soak up some moon rays. I'll let you know when they arrive."

"Thanks."

April climbed in the back and grabbed a cushion from off the parcel shelf. She lay down and closed her eyes. Within minutes, she was asleep and snoring quietly.

Six

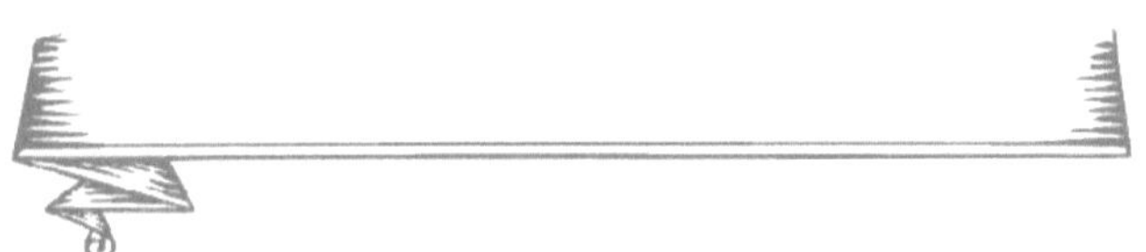

Briella woke April when the clean-up crew arrived and they went through the same process as last time.

"Excuse me, April," Jared, the head cleaner called, "this one is still alive."

April raced over to take a look. She shone Jared's torch over the victim's eyes to reveal irises that had turned dark. "Jared, this one has the DNA sequence. He must be blessed and cremated at once. Don't let him bite you or the change will quicken and his strength will double," she warned.

"Is she creating new vampires?"

"Looks like it. He must have tasted her blood."

Jared got on the phone and made arrangements for the immediate cleansing of the man's soul. Once April's responsibility to the deceased had been fulfilled, she marked the map with their current location and drew an imaginary line between the two sites.

Now that she had a starting point to begin her search, April and Briella drove to the mid-point and began the tedious task of looking for anything out of the ordinary. If the vampire was who she said she was, April didn't like her chances of finding any clues to the whereabouts of her temporary lair.

April pulled up in a shopping centre carpark. The sky lightened quickly as the sun peered over the horizon. "Great, there goes our chance of picking up on her brainwaves," April told Briella.

"Um, April, there is something I need to tell you." April looked at her quizzically. "This vampire seems to be able to block herself from us."

"I don't understand. How could she do that?" April quizzed.

"I'm not sure. All I know is that both times I tracked her, there was a period where she just disappeared and suddenly reappeared kilometres away, many minutes later."

"What are you saying? That she can be just as dead to us during the night as she is when she sleeps during the day."

"I am afraid so."

"No vampire has been able to do that before," April complained.

"April, I don't think this is your average, everyday vampire."

"It certainly looks that way, doesn't it? I hope Sophia gets back to me quickly with the information I requested. Perhaps you had better go home, Briella. I'm not sure you should be anywhere near this vampire. Who knows what she would become if she were to get hold of your fairy magic."

"My job is to locate the creatures and I haven't been able to do that yet. There are no creatures on the grid that don't already have a Locator tracking them. I am not leaving you because you are frightened of something that may never happen."

April knew when Briella dug in her heels, nothing she said or did would change her mind. She grabbed her handbag and asked Briella to fly inside. Briella placed the headset on the parcel shelf and then took up her place inside the bag. The pair would need to communicate through mind-link from now on.

The place they had pulled up in was definitely not as busy as the coastal towns April usually worked in, but neither was it as quiet as the country towns where her friend, Force, frequented. April wasn't sure how the people in this town dressed so she decided to stick with her shirt, pants and boots. If she generated stares of an uncomfortable nature, she would change her attire to something more suitable. They walked the streets for half an hour before they came across the first couple of humans going for their morning walk. Friendly greetings were said in passing and Briella said how thankful she was to have been given Australia as her base of operations.

Briella didn't have any knowledge of the other continents she could have been placed on other than what she learned from watching the migrants who came to live here. They were just as friendly, but April never bothered to point that out to her. It wouldn't make any difference to the way Briella viewed things. They hadn't been given a choice in where they were sent and in the three thousand years they had been here as Earth's protectors, they had never been moved around the planet once.

April decided to find a hotel that had a vacant room for rent. They would need somewhere to base themselves while they were there. A hotel room would give them an opportunity to bathe and have healthy meals prepared for them rather than having to shop and cook food themselves. They had fourteen hours before the vampire would rise from her sleep. April was not confident they would be able to find her in that time. They didn't even know if the mid-point was actually the area in which she slept. She might have gone twenty kilometres one way and eighty the other. It would give them something to do until Briella was able to pick her up again. Perhaps they would strike it lucky.

Gemma dressed quickly for school and ran into Bastian's room to check on him. His head felt hot and his eyes looked feverish.

"How you doing, Bastian?" she asked quietly.

"I don't feel so good this morning, Gem. You might have to go on the bus without me."

"Ah, don't worry about me, Bas. I'm a big girl who can take care of herself *and* her big brother. You just get better, okay?"

Gemma ran to the bathroom to get a clean cup out of the cupboard above the sink. She filled it with water and grabbed a washer from the linen cupboard and placed it under the tap. Gemma carried them back into her brother's room. She helped him take small sips of water until he indicated he had enough. Then she placed the washer over his forehead.

"I'll be back before you know it. Get some sleep." She checked the bite marks on his neck. They had nearly disappeared. Gemma ran downstairs to the kitchen for breakfast. While she ate, she handed her mother a shopping list full of items she required 'for school' the next day.

"Cloves of garlic, wood stakes crafted from the Aspen tree, eight crosses and a silver necklace. What do you need all this for? Have you decided to go to vampire school?" Karen questioned with a laugh.

"Mum, be serious. We are doing a play at school and I want to look as authentic as I can, playing the slayer of vampires."

"You never mentioned this to me before," Karen replied.

"I have been so caught up in trying to improve my English and history writing, I forgot to check my diary to see what was coming up," Gemma countered.

"And you realised your error in judgement this morning and you require these items for tomorrow." Gemma nodded her head in agreement. "Mrs Talbot didn't send a letter or email saying you were doing a play and might need to make or purchase some props."

"Well, it's in my diary, so we must be," Gemma said becoming upset. If her mother didn't buy her the items, how was she going to protect Bastian from the vampire across the street?

"It's okay, honey, don't get upset. I'll pick them up on my way home from work this afternoon."

VAMPIRE

"Thanks, Mum," Gemma said with a sigh of relief as she continued feeding her face. As soon as she arrived home from school, Gemma would set about trapping the vampire in Mr. Cameron's house and save her brother from being its next meal, or worse, becoming one of them.

The school day was long and Gemma barely remembered anything about the lessons the teachers presented. She wanted desperately to tell her best friend Katherine about the vampire at lunchtime, but didn't for fear of placing her life in danger, too.

She wondered how Bastian was doing. Had the vampire given him some kind of infection that he would never recover from? Had the process of becoming one of them already begun? Would she discover that her brother had become a monster that thirsted for her blood when sunset occurred?

Gemma kept her eye on the clock which seemed to move more slowly than usual. She couldn't wait for the home bell to ring so she could begin the vampire-proofing. She just hoped it wasn't too late for her brother. Gemma wondered if there was any point in asking her Mum to take him to the doctor. They wouldn't know what was wrong with him and probably wouldn't have a clue how to fix him either.

Gemma had gone to the library during lunch to see if she could find any plays on vampires in case her mother asked for more details, but couldn't find any. Mrs Talbot was a bit weird and she didn't feel like bringing her current interest in vampires to Mrs Talbot's attention. It wouldn't do for her teacher and mother to begin a discussion over a non-existent play. Gemma decided she would tell her mother the class was writing the play together as a group and would then perform it for assessment purposes. 'Yes, that would work,' she thought.

She managed to make it through the afternoon classes and was packed up and ready to leave five minutes before the bell. As soon as she heard its chimes, she was out the door and first in line for the bus home.

Seven

Gemma checked on Bastian as soon as she arrived home. His fever had broken and his eyes looked clearer than they did that morning. "Hey, Kiddo, how was school?" he asked her, sitting up in bed.

"Fine, you know how school is," she replied.

"No maths or science today then?" he questioned.

"That would be correct," she grimaced. "Are you hungry? Can I get you anything to eat?" she asked, hoping he wasn't beginning to thirst for blood.

"Do you think you could ask Mum for some chicken soup?"

"Is she home sick, too?"

"No, the boss gave her the afternoon off."

"I'll ask now," she replied giving him a hug. "Can I get you a drink as well?"

"Now that you mention it I am a bit parched. How about a lovely tall glass of water with a few ice cubes thrown in?"

"You got it, Bastian. I am glad you are feeling better," Gemma said, as she skipped out of the room to find her mother.

"Hi, Mum, how was your day?" she asked finding her in the lounge room.

"Good thanks, Love. How was yours?"

"Good. Bastian would like some chicken soup if you can manage it," Gemma stated, as she headed for the kitchen to organise his drink.

Karen walked into the room and smiled as Gemma busily poured cooled water over the ice cubes she had placed in the glass.

"Wow, someone's thirsty," Karen remarked, getting a tin of soup out of the cupboard.

"Yeah, Bastian. This is for him."

"I hope he appreciates what a wonderful sister you are."

"You bet he does. Bastian is awesome," Gemma said, turning around and seeing the can of soup on the bench. "Aren't you going to make it from scratch?"

"I don't have any fresh chicken. Would you like me to go back to the shops to buy some?"

"No, that won't be necessary. Did you get a chance to get those items for *me*?"

"Yes, Gemma, I did. They are on your desk."

"Thanks, Mum," Gemma said planting a kiss on her cheek. "Do you need a hand with anything?"

"Yes, you can wait for this to heat up, and then take it up to Bastian for me," Karen said, placing the bowl filled with soup into the microwave.

Gemma grinned at her mother. "I intended on taking it up to him, with that," she said pointing to the glass.

The microwave beeped and Gemma took out the bowl. She placed it on a tray with some cutlery and the glass of water, then carried it up the stairs. After placing the tray on his lap, she made her excuses to leave. Gemma was eager to begin erecting the crosses on the four major magnetic points of their house and Mr. Cameron's across the street. She hoped to keep the vampire trapped and failing that, keep the vampire out of theirs. The garlic would be strung across all windows on the lower floor. Gemma would love to cover the windows on the upper levels as well but she was afraid of heights. Besides, there wouldn't be enough time or garlic to do both houses before nightfall.

Her biggest fear was her family inviting the vampire in. Gemma wasn't sure how she would stop them if the vampire arrived on their doorstep. She would just have to hope the crosses and garlic worked by keeping her imprisoned in the house until she could find a way of getting rid of her.

As she checked out the haul, she noticed her mother had not gotten the wood from the Aspen tree. Gemma hadn't really expected her to be able to find the proper stuff anyway. She was thrilled that her mother had bought some balsa wood to create the crosses. It might not be able to kill the vampire in the event of an attack, but it should certainly help to keep the vampire at a distance once she had put them into the form of a cross.

The necklace was a simple silver chain. It was probably too fine to be considered manly, but Gemma would try to talk Bastian into wearing it anyway. It might prevent the vampire from taking another bite. Gemma was a little naïve in these types of matters and never considered there were other parts of the body that could be bitten.

Placing the items in her bag, Gemma snuck down the stairs and into the garage where her father kept his tools. She seized a hammer and a packet of nails to place the crosses on the walls and doors; some fishing line to thread the garlic on, to hang from the windows; and some plastic flowers that her mother had not liked, to disguise the cloves of garlic from passers-by.

She set to work and was kept busy for the next couple of hours. Her father came home, took one look at Gemma's activities and went to find Karen.

"Can you tell me what is going on out there?"

"Hi, Honey. I'm fine, thank you. How was your day?" Karen answered.

"Sorry, Love. All of the above," he said, giving her a quick kiss on the lips. "I am hoping you know what Gemma is up to and have approved her actions."

"What are you talking about, Love? Gemma is upstairs doing her homework or keeping Bastian company. I am not sure which."

"Your beautiful, intelligent, inquisitive daughter is outside stringing stuff across the windows of Carl's place."

"You're kidding me," Karen spluttered.

VAMPIRE

"I kid you not," Walter replied with a grimace.

Karen hurried to the front door and saw her busy, determined daughter for herself. "She told me that stuff was for school. Why is she putting it all over Carl's place?"

"I don't know, Love. That is what I have been asking you."

Karen and Walter crossed the street to question their daughter. "Why are you putting crosses and flowers on Carl's place?"

"I did it to our own as well," Gemma replied stalling so she could give a very good explanation for her behaviour.

"Sarina is going to be displeased to see you have defaced her home when she wakes to go to work," Walter informed her.

"My hammering woke Sarina up and she came over to investigate. I told her we were doing a play at school about vampires and I wanted to get into character as the slayer of vampires. She thought it was a great idea to decorate my home as that would probably be what a slayer of vampires would do. Then she suggested that I decorated her house, too, because I wouldn't be able to see our home from inside, but would be able to see hers every time I looked out a window."

"Why do both our children take things to the extreme?" Karen complained to Walter. "Bastian is an Olympic contender and Gemma always has to take her projects to the highest level possible."

"They get it from you, Love," Walter replied, wrapping his arm around her waist. "You are the most driven person in our entire family."

Karen looked at him sheepishly in agreement. "Would you like a hand?" she asked Gemma.

"No thanks, Mum. It would defeat the purpose of getting into character. I can't wait to show you the script when I finish it."

"We can't wait to read it," Karen and Walter replied in unison.

"I'll be finished putting up the props in about twenty minutes. Any chance I could have a hot chocolate when I'm done?" Gemma asked, batting her eyelashes.

"Of course you can," Karen replied.

"Be careful with those tools," Walter reminded her.

"I'm not a little kid, Dad!"

"No, you are right. You are a teenager, after all. Well, we'll leave you to it then."

Gemma toiled as quickly as she could without jeopardising the quality of her work. Once she had completed her task, she grabbed her cup of hot chocolate from the kitchen bench and went upstairs to find Bastian.

She knocked on the door and found him sitting on the corner of his desk. "What are you doing?" It was obvious he wasn't cleaning it off, as everything was in the same place it was that morning, when she had checked on him.

"I've been watching you. What are you doing, Gem?" He looked at her with eyes that told her he would know if she lied.

"I am protecting you from that vampire across the street," she replied truthfully.

"You're what?" he asked cackling.

"Shhh, you'll bring Mum and Dad in. Take a look at your neck. She bit you last night."

Bastian humoured her and took a look. There was nothing there. No bite marks or scars. It was completely normal. He turned around and looked at her enquiringly.

"That's impossible," she stated. "I saw the marks there myself. You came home and walked up the stairs like a zombie. You didn't answer me when I asked if you were all right and I could see the marks on your neck. They were there!" she yelled at him, while he looked at her like she had lost her mind.

"Now who's going to have Mum and Dad running," he said placing his arm around her shoulder.

"You were so sick this morning, I thought she may have given you some deadly disease or sucked out too much of your blood. I even got scared you were going to die, or worse, turn into one of them yourself."

"That's not going to happen, Kiddo. I promise."

"Are you going to see her again?"

"I might."

"Then don't make promises you can't keep," she pouted, and moved to leave the room.

"Gemma ...."

"I don't want to talk about it anymore. You are my brother and I love you with all my heart, but I will never forgive you if you allow her to kill you. Or worse."

Gemma left the room and went to her own, slamming the door. She realised she had left the hot chocolate in Bastian's room but didn't want to go back in there to collect it. Gemma checked the time on her clock, set her alarm and lay down on the bed. Sunset was still a couple of hours away. She was an emotional wreck and the tears began to fall as she thought about what she was up against.

Gemma was so young and the vampire was probably two hundred years old. She closed her eyes to try to stop the tears from welling and fell asleep. It was going to be another long night watching the house across the street, but this time, it would be to see if her protective measures worked.

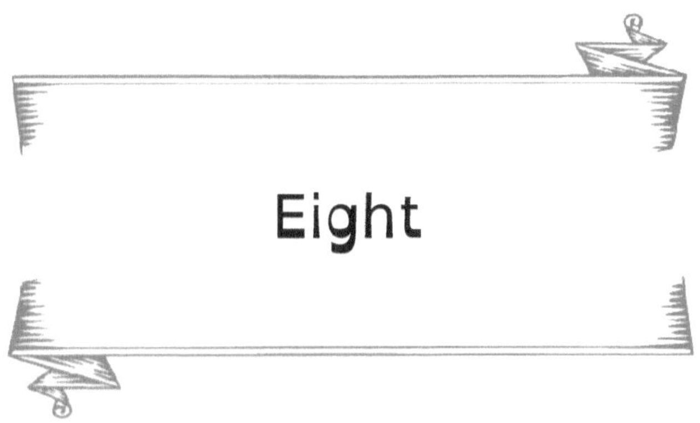

Eight

The beeping of the alarm roused Gemma from her sleep. It took a while for the confusion to clear and her thoughts to focus on her mission: to see if the protective measures she had put in place had the vampire trapped inside Mr Cameron's home. Gemma scurried off the bed and moved to her desk by the window.

She sat on her chair and pulled the curtains back so she could view the house across the street.

Her mother called her for dinner, which she ignored. There was no way she was taking her eyes off the house so early. Nightfall was minutes away and she hoped the vampire would try to leave as soon as the light disappeared. Gemma didn't have much experience with vampires. She wasn't one of those children who were interested in such things.

The little that she had learned from the internet told her that vampires fell asleep when the sun came up and woke as soon as it went down. Other than that, it didn't really explain what they did with their time except drink the blood of humans. Based on that, Gemma was pretty certain the vampire would want to leave the house as soon as it woke.

"Didn't you hear me calling?" Karen asked.

"Sorry, Mother, I'm not feeling very well. Would it be okay if I ate my dinner in my room, just for tonight?"

Karen came in and placed her hand on Gemma's forehead. "You don't feel hot," she stated.

"I don't feel flu sick. Just yuck in the tummy. I would like to be close to the bathroom if my stomach decides to expel its contents," Gemma said.

"Well, when you put it that way, sounds like a great idea to me. I'll have Bastian bring it up."

"Is he feeling better?" Gemma asked, upset that she had forgotten to check on him.

"Yes, honey. He tells me he is feeling great now," Karen replied and left the room.

Gemma felt hopeful that Bastian really was okay and that the vampire hadn't infected him with anything. She turned her face to the window to watch the house across the road. The vampire wasn't going to sneak past her if she could help it. The last of the light faded to darkness, and Gemma waited with bated breath. She almost jumped through the window when Bastian placed her dinner in front of her.

"Oh my God, Bastian. What are you doing sneaking up on me like that?" Gemma squealed in fright.

"I didn't sneak. You seemed to be concentrating pretty hard. What were you thinking?" he enquired.

Gemma thought fast and said, "I was trying to work out whether it was better to eat and then throw up or not eat at all. But then I started to think by thinking about it, I might throw up anyway."

"Not feeling well then," Bastian said placing his hand on her forehead.

"Mum's already done that," Gemma said rolling her eyes.

"Why are you staring out the window?" he asked. "You usually look at me when we're talking to one another."

"I'm just not feeling well, Bastian. Please don't make me feel worse."

"I'm sorry, Kiddo. Do you want me to stay with you?"

"No thanks. Actually, I would rather be on my own," she replied.

"I'll come back later and collect your plate. Can I get you anything else?"

"Some dry ginger ale would be good if we have any. It helps to settle my stomach."

"Okay, beautiful. Back soon. Oh, by the way, has your garlic and crosses kept the vampire in the house?"

"Thought you didn't believe she was a vampire?"

"I don't, but you do."

"No, she hasn't left yet," Gemma advised.

Gemma picked at her food. She had told her family a lie about being ill, and yet the worry the vampire was causing her was actually beginning to make her feel sick. "Come on, Gem, stop being so God damned psychosomatic," she said aloud. "Oh great, now you are offending God and you are going to need him to give you a hand with getting rid of this dangerous creature," she continued. Gemma said a prayer to appease God and his angels and continued to keep watch.

She sat that way for two hours until her bodily functions screamed for her to take a break. Before she went to the bathroom, she set her phone to record video, in case the vampire chose that particular time to leave the dwelling. That was if she could get past the crosses and garlic.

When Gemma got back to her window she tried to keep one eye on Mr. Cameron's house and the other on the video before her. As far as she could tell, the vampire was still in the house. She had no way of knowing whether that was by choice or inability to leave. Gemma also had no idea that Sarina would have been able to leave the house completely unseen, if that was what Sarina wished, due to the speed at which she moved. Unbeknownst to Gemma, while she watched the house across the street for any signs of movement, she herself was being watched.

VAMPIRE

Sarina sat at the dining room table in the dark. From there, she was able to see Gemma sitting at her desk, believing she was hidden from view. She watched Bastian bring her food and turn the light on when he left her room. She also watched as Gemma picked at her food and then walked backwards to the light switch, placing herself in darkness once more.

The darkness didn't matter. Sarina could see her perfectly, even from that distance. She watched the girl and at times felt like Gemma was looking straight at her. Of course, Sarina knew the girl couldn't see her with her pathetic human eyes. She wondered what the girl was thinking and figured it had something to do with the steps she had taken to protect her family, while she thought Sarina had been dead to the world.

As an ancient vampire, Sarina was able to wake during daylight hours. Sarina had never thought of turning a child. She had always found them to be terribly painful to be around. This child, however, was different. Maybe this one would make a lovely addition to her family and would make her new love happy.

The crosses and garlic would not stop her from leaving when the time came. She would be there to greet her love and turn him. April had better make sure he was there or all hell would break loose. Sarina had all night to watch the girl. She wouldn't sleep until the sun came up in the morning. Sarina was interested to see how long Gemma could make herself stay awake in order to protect her brother.

Sarina wasn't particularly in a playful mood. She toyed with the idea of calling to Bastian so that he would come to her and she could see what Gemma's response would be. Now that she was considering changing Gemma, she realised it would be better to orchestrate their first meeting when Bastian wasn't around.

'Imagine the evilness of feeding Gemma's brother to her as her first meal,' Sarina thought.

Pity she wasn't here for evil's sake. She had decided to give Bastian to her new mate as a gift and wasn't about to change her mind now. Sarina thought of another time she had changed her mind and it had led to the death of her husband, Karayan. Her eyes watched Gemma but her mind was somewhere else.

For three thousand years they had been imprisoned on the planet, Mystique. The Battle Stars thought they were doing the creatures a favour and in some ways, she supposed they had. They were unable to leave the land created for them, hence the imprisonment, but none of them went hungry, though they weren't able to hunt their own food.

The land they were assigned to remained in darkness most of the time. Every couple of centuries, a solar event brought sunlight to their home for a couple of hours. The royals from the Land of Beginnings had organised a castle be built to provide protection for Sarina, Karayan, and their family A clock that warned of the impending solar event gave them plenty of time to seek the protection of the castle.

They were told that none of their kind would be harmed as long as they didn't harm any of the Battle Stars that came to their land. So an uneasy truce came into being and kept the members of each side safe, most of the time. On occasions, Battle Stars would attempt to steal their artefacts or test their theories on the methods required to kill vampires. That led to conflicts between the jailers and the inmates, which sometimes led to death.

It would have been easier to accept the death of her beloved had it been under one of those circumstances. That would have been a hero's death and his name would have become a legend with time. Karayan's death was the result of some stupid Battle Star who was too damned trigger happy with his fire finger. Sarina would have loved to place all the blame at the foot of the Blazer that took his life, but felt most of the responsibility lay with herself.

VAMPIRE

Adair had told her a new team of Battle Stars was being sent to their land to learn the art of negotiation. This was one of the skills required to advance to the level of Custodian. Adair had asked that both Sarina and Karayan be present at the meeting to facilitate the safety of the Battle Star team.

A Battle Star team consisted of six members: a Dampier who controls water, a Mucker who controls the soil, a Blazer who controls fire, a Shifter who can change their image to take on the shape of any living thing, a Minder who can influence another by communicating mind-to-mind, and a Natural who cares for the fauna and flora of the planet. Adair was interested in their opinions as to whether the team had acquired the mandatory skill set to be effective as future negotiators, for the benefit of the creatures that existed on the planet.

They hadn't. To be fairer to the team, their Blazer hadn't. When Karayan became a bit animated during their discussions, the Blazer had retreated to the use of his elemental power instead of enabling his newfound power over language. The Blazer's fire can become hot enough to cremate any creature without leaving behind any remnants under certain circumstances. It is an instinctual event that cannot be created on a conscious level. The Blazer's fear of Karayan had brought forth this crematory blast and without the blood of his creator, Sarina, Karayan was not able to heal from the burning.

The actions of the team's Dampier was able to put out the flames but was not quick enough to prevent them from reaching their mark in the first place. Karayan died in front of the seven members of Sarina and Karayan's executive team of vampires, who would have loved to have retaliated but were unable to because they had not been given approval by Sarina. That gave the Battle Stars time to flee the Land of Darkness, unchallenged, and return to the safety of their own land. Queen Adair was very apologetic, but her words would never make up for the loss suffered by Sarina.

Sarina noticed movement, which brought her out of her reverie. Gemma had finally succumbed to sleep. She looked at the watch on her arm, two o'clock. Perhaps she would have a different kind of fun tonight. Sarina exited the house without any issues from the ornaments Gemma had placed on the doors and the windows. She made her way to the veranda outside Bastian's room and tapped on the window with her claws. She waited patiently for him to appear.

"Sarina," he said groggily with sleep, "is everything okay?"

"Everything is fine, Bastian. May I come in?"

"How come you are not at work?" he questioned.

"They rang me to say there had been a mix-up with the roster and I am not meant to start until tomorrow night. Are we going to stay out here all night?"

"Oh, sorry, come on in," Bastian replied.

Sarina walked inside and sat on the corner of his desk.

"I've been a bit busy with school and gymnastics. My desk doesn't usually look like that," he stated with embarrassment.

"I didn't come over here to see how clean or messy you are, Bastian," Sarina replied.

"Why did you come?" Bastian asked expectantly.

"I suppose you know your sister thinks I am a vampire." As Bastian nodded his head in agreement, Sarina continued, "I wanted to know if you do, too."

"Of course not. There is no such thing," he replied.

"*Good. Hop into bed, Bastian,*" Sarina said with her hypnotic style of communication. When he complied, she added, "*You will tell Gemma about our conversation over breakfast in the morning. Now, go to sleep.*"

Sarina left the same way she came in. Now that he had invited her in, she would be able to come and go as she pleased. Gemma was going to have a nasty surprise in the morning if she had done her homework.

Sarina had learned how to use the internet when she had bitten Bastian and it had been surprising to see the amount of information she had been able to gather on her kind. More astounding was how accurate most of the material online had been. Sarina didn't know about the inability to enter a dwelling without being invited in and was surprised to see that she had been unable to enter Bastian's of her own volition.

Sarina made her way back to Carl's and settled back down at the dining room table. She watched Gemma sleep at her desk until just before sunrise, when she made her way to the back of the house to sleep out the day.

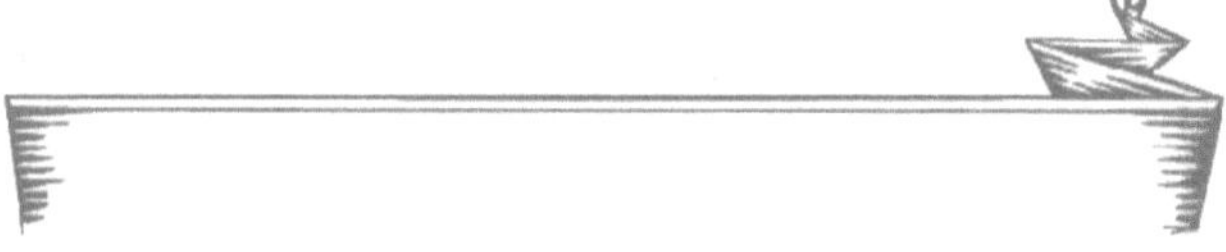

Nine

Gemma woke up with a sore neck. She tried to stretch out the kinks but it hurt too much. There was no movement across the road, but then Gemma didn't expect there to be. Vampires slept during the day. She was disappointed in herself for falling asleep and had no idea how long she had been out for. She could only hope the garlic and crosses had done their job and the vampire had found herself trapped inside.

Unfortunately, Bastian burst that little bubble when she arrived at the breakfast table.

"Hey, Gem, how's things?" Bastian said.

"Great, how are you feeling this morning? Any relapses?" she asked.

"Not a one. What time did you get to sleep?"

"I don't know, late. But I didn't see the vamp leave the house," Gemma smirked.

"Well, she did."

"How do you know? Did you see her leave?" Gemma squealed distressed.

"She turned up in my bedroom. She knows that you think she is a vampire and she wanted to know if I thought so, too."

"You let her in, didn't you?"

"Sure, she's not dangerous, Gem, and she is not a vampire."

Gemma ran out of the room and burst into tears. She couldn't understand why her brother didn't believe her. 'How could *he* have *let her in?* ' she asked herself, but knew the answer.

Hormones. He liked her, even if she was a bloodthirsty creature of the dark that lusted after blood, and would probably end up turning him into one of the living dead.

She flew up the staircase and slammed the door to the bathroom. Gemma pulled out her toothbrush and cleaned her teeth. There was no point in trying to finish her breakfast as she had lost her appetite. She was about to exit the bathroom when her mother knocked on the door.

"Are you okay, Gemma?"

"Yes, I'll be out in a minute."

"Any reason you slammed the door?"

"No, it just slipped in my hands. I'm sorry, Mother, it won't happen again."

Gemma was pleased to hear her mother moving away from the door. She flushed the toilet to give her a reason for being in there for so long and splashed her face to wash away the tears. Back in her room, Gemma put on her uniform, packed her bag and ran down the stairs, yelling goodbye to her mother as she left the house.

"What's up with Gemma this morning?" Karen asked Bastian. "She wasn't well last night and now she has left without eating her breakfast or packing her lunch."

"I'm not sure," Bastian replied, "but I can take her lunch and give it to her on the bus."

"Should I be worried about her?"

"No, Gemma's okay. She's just at that awkward age. All her friends are a little bit weird at the moment," Bastian advised his mother.

"You mean they've finally noticed how 'nice' Gemma's older brother is," Karen said knowingly.

"Yeah, Mum. Something like that," Bastian laughed.

He grabbed the lunches and strode to his room. Bastian dressed quickly, packed his bag and headed to the bus stop himself. He wished he hadn't told Gemma about Sarina's visit and couldn't quite understand why it had rushed out of his mouth like it had. When Bastian caught up to her, he tried to apologise but she wouldn't listen to him. She placed her hands over her ears and made childish noises. Bastian didn't want Gemma to embarrass herself further so he placed her lunch in her bag then walked to the other end of the shelter.

The ride to school was uneventful. Bastian sat up the back with the seniors and Gemma sat down the front with the juniors. When they arrived at school, Gemma bounced off the bus and rushed through the front gates. Bastian didn't get to talk to her again until they were home. He tried to find her at lunch but she had gone to the library with her best friend, Katherine. The librarians wouldn't let the seniors and the juniors mix together. It did wonders to prevent a lot of bullying issues within the school but didn't help with circumstances such as this.

He saw her sitting in a cubicle down the back and felt a bit more comfortable after seeing her laugh. He wished he knew what they had been talking about. He was sure he saw her mouth the word 'vampire'.

"You've been looking sad all morning, Gemma. What's wrong?" Katherine asked.

"You wouldn't believe me if I told you," Gemma stated with a sigh.

"Try me," Katherine replied softly.

Gemma took a few seconds to contemplate her options. Katherine was a very good friend who would never make fun of Gemma on purpose. They had been friends for a long time. They were similar in stature, but Katherine was a lot fairer in hair and skin colour than Gemma. Her eyes were pale blue which seemed a bit off-putting to those who met her for the first time. Katherine tucked her hair behind her ear while she waited patiently for Gemma to decide whether or not to disclose her worries.

"A vampire has moved in across the road," Gemma whispered.

"Holy crap, are you sure?" Katherine squealed.

"Keep it down and watch your language, Miss Katherine," the Junior Librarian said sternly.

"Sorry, Mrs B!" Then more quietly, Katherine asked, "How do you know it's a vampire?"

"She's got my brother wrapped around her little finger and he came home the night before last with fang marks on his neck."

"What are you going to do?"

"I don't know. I put crosses on the doors and hung garlic on the windows, but it still left the house and came over to ours."

"You didn't let it in, did you?"

"No, my brother did. How am I supposed to protect him from himself?"

"I don't know but it knows you are on to it. Gemma, I hate to say this, but you have probably made it really mad."

"So, you believe me then?" Gemma asked incredulously.

"Of course. My brother, Tommy, and I, were being tormented by a Bogeyman. Callum, from Starlight Investigations, helped protect us from the monster and sent it where it could never hurt anyone ever again. I think we should give them a call."

Katherine pulled her phone out of her pocket and rang the number she had pre-programmed for an emergency such as this. It wasn't long before a voice came on the line.

"Hello, Starlight Investigations. You are talking to Samuel. Please state your name and age."

"My name is Katherine and I'm fifteen years old. My friend, Gemma, is living across the road from a vampire and needs assistance."

"How did you become aware of Starlight Investigations?"

"I have had previous dealings with Callum."

"Is your friend currently with you?"

"Yes, she's right beside me."

"Can you put her on the phone, please?"

"He wants to talk to you," Katherine said as she handed the phone to Gemma.

"Hello, Gemma speaking."

"Gemma, this is Samuel. Please state your residential address, contact number and any details you can give me on the vampire."

"Is this guy serious or are you pranking me?" Gemma asked with her hand over the phone to mute her voice.

"He's for real, talk to him, Gemma. He can help."

Gemma gave her address and phone number and then discussed the details of the vampire.

"Well, it's a young female that made our neighbour, Mr. Cameron, leave two nights ago. She bit my brother on the neck, but he hasn't turned or anything. I saw the marks on his neck when he came home but they were practically gone in the morning. How does that even happen?" she wailed.

"Have you seen anyone coming or going?"

"What do you mean?"

"Does she have a human companion with her?" Samuel questioned.

"No, there are no humans over there," Gemma advised.

"Does she know you know what she is?"

"Yes. I put crosses on her doors and garlic on her windows, but it didn't work. She came over to our house last night and my brother invited her in. I guess we are all doomed now."

"Gemma, I want you to listen very carefully. Do not go over there. Do not put any more things on the house. Stay away from her and if you can, ask your brother to rescind the invitation to your home. I will have someone over there as soon as possible to remove the problem for you. Thank you for your call and have a nice day."

Samuel hung up on his end and contacted April, whom he knew was tracking the vampire. He called up the file on the computer to ascertain what information Sophia had been able to assemble and discovered the Queen herself had replied to Sophia's enquiries.

Sarina, Queen of the Vampires, has escaped the confines of her land and has somehow managed to travel to Earth via the portal. She is to be handled with extreme caution. Being one of the ancients, she is exceptionally powerful and dangerous. Any Gatherers currently tracking the vampire are to desist immediately. Advise you contact Toranthian, the Gatherer responsible for her previous capture, to tend to the situation and resolve the issue.

"Hello, April. I have some information that is of great consequence to your current case," he began.

"Thank the Lord, Samuel. I've just spent the past twenty four hours combing the streets, looking like a crim trying to find an easy target, in an attempt to discover the lair that vamp has bunkered down in."

"That kind of talk is totally inappropriate, April. Queen Adair has confirmed the Queen of the Vampires has indeed escaped to Earth. I have sent the address she is currently using, and the name of the owner to your phone.

"The house across the street has a fifteen-year-old girl named Gemma, who has advised that she has attempted to take protective measures against the vampire. I believe her life to be in imminent danger. We have been advised to contact Toranthian, the Gatherer who originally captured Sarina. He will be taking over the case. I can connect you to a conference call with Toranthian so that you can pass on pertinent information."

"What do you mean Toren is taking over the case? I am quite capable of dealing with a vampire, Samuel."

"You have been given an instruction by the Queen, April. You are to do nothing towards capturing the vampire. Your only concern is to protect the family across the street. Are you planning on defying your orders?"

"No, of course not," April said with anger.

"Connecting you now," Samuel advised. "I have Toranthian on the line, you may communicate now," he said and hung up.

"Hi, April. What's up?" Toranthian enquired.

"Hi, Toren. I have a situation here and need your help. The Queen of the Vampires has escaped from Mystique and made her way here."

"Wait, what? Sarina is back on Earth?" he spluttered.

"Yeah, and it's pretty bad. She has already killed over thirty people in one night and has stated that if you are not in the Gold Coast's Hinterlands by eight o'clock tonight, she will slaughter a thousand people by dawn."

"I've got a friend that has a chopper who can get me there in a couple of hours. Have you got any gear, or do I need to bring some with me?"

"Nah, I've got everything you need. I'll text you the address. See you in a couple of hours," she said dejectedly. April didn't want him anywhere near Sarina. The Queen of the Vampires had requested his presence so she must have some kind of evil scheme planned for him. After talking to him, she was reminded again how nice the guy was. Under any other circumstances, April would have been ecstatic to have been able to spend a few hours with him and catch up with what's been happening down south.

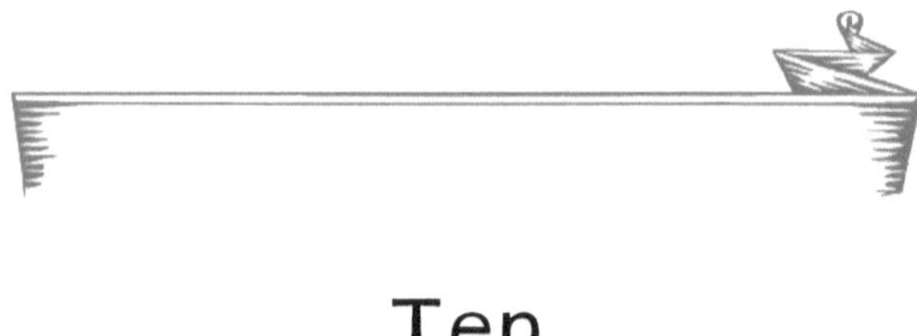

Ten

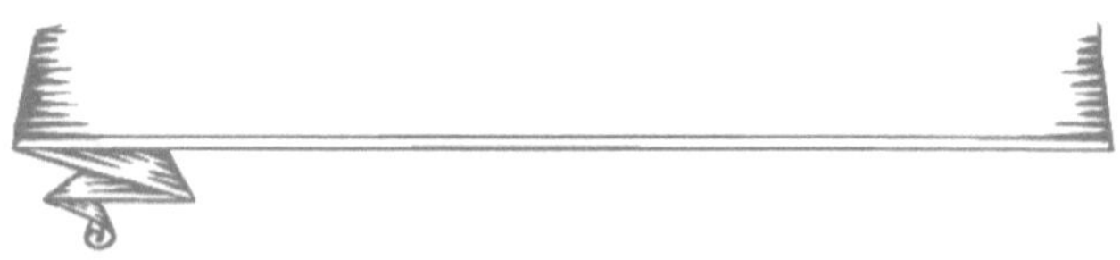

Briella flew into April's handbag so she could get from the hotel room April had rented, to the car without being seen by the humans. Once inside, she collected the headset from the parcel shelf and perched herself on the steering wheel facing April. After turning it on and hearing the radio crackle to life she asked April what their next course of action was.

"Samuel has ordered me to disengage with the vampire."

"Why?" Briella interjected. "It will be asleep and you won't be in any danger. You could place the net of silver over her without incident and the Collectors could come and take her away. Problem solved."

"Yes, I know. But they have told me to stand down. Toren is required to handle the capturing of this vampire."

"But there is no need for Toren to be placed in peril."

"The vamp more or less told me she was brought here by Queen Adair. If she was telling the truth, then the Queen obviously knows the reason why she is here and it has something to do with Toren."

"Or the Queen is asking that he assists you because he is the one who originally captured her for relocation," Briella reminded her.

"He is not assisting me, Briella, he is taking over."

"How are they even going to know if you help him out a little?"

April gave Briella an incredulous stare. Was she encouraging her to go against orders? "How did she get on Earth in the first place, Briella, and why is she here on her own? Surely if she had come up with a plan to escape Mystique, she would have brought the rest of the vampires with her."

"Hmm, you have a great point there, April. Perhaps Toren can shed some light when he arrives. Having dealt with her before, he can tell us what she was like the last time she was here. Maybe she doesn't give a hoot about her kind. Sarina might only be concerned about her own wants and needs."

"Wouldn't you think that if the Queen of the Vampires had escaped on her own, our Queen would have sent a hunting party of Guardians?"

"April, it is not up to us to second guess our Queen. She *is* our ruler and we are *supposed* to do as commanded."

There it was again. A suggestion that they break the rules. "I know. You're right. We'll go check out the place Sarina has taken for her own. By the time we do that, the kid across the street should be getting home from school and we can have a chat with her about what she has seen."

"And then it shouldn't be long before we see that hunky man of a Gatherer turn up on our doorstep," Briella said rubbing her hands together.

"Oh my goodness, Briella. You are going to have me crash into something when you do things like that," April giggled. "You know he has been dating Rochelle for only about *five centuries*."

"That doesn't mean I can't appreciate his beauty."

They drove the rest of the way in silence. Briella had turned to face the windscreen so she could check out the landscape. April liked to live and work in the city. She preferred the hustle and bustle that a larger population brought to an area and realised that most creatures were drawn to that type of environment. She was also a workaholic and loved that there was not a lot of downtime between cases in the city.

April was not very good at sitting still. She didn't care to take leisurely strolls along the beach or to dine alfresco on a warm summer's night. April enjoyed the manual tasks of separating a victim from its tormentor. For this reason, Briella spent most of her time amongst the skyscrapers and built up areas of South-East Queensland. She thought it was nice to see some space between homes and huge expanses of greenery for a change.

April slowed down to match the speed limit and looked at the navigation screen to locate the address Samuel had given her. After weaving her way through the housing estate, she came to a stop outside Gemma's home. It was a nice area and the homes in the street were twice as large as the apartment April currently lived in.

April opened her handbag for Briella to hide in once she had returned her headphones to the rear of the car. Briella flew in quickly and nestled herself inside. She hated having to hide every time she was around the humans, but it had been proven time and time again that humans could not be trusted with the knowledge that fairies were real.

"I can't see anybody around, Briella. I am going to walk the perimeter of the vamps house to find the exit points."

The house was constructed with bricks that had been rendered in a pale grey colour. There were large, white bay windows in every room on the lower floor with at least two sets of French doors on all four sides.

This house was going to be a nightmare to batten down if Toren was held up for any reason and did not arrive until after nightfall. There was no way April and Briella would be able to cover all the exits and Sarina would have no trouble getting away.

April checked the boot of the car and found she had three nets that would cover one and a half windows. Not nearly enough to get the job done. They were designed to contain the creature, not a structure, but April, being the resourceful soul that she was, thought she would take a look anyway to see what she could come up with in a pinch.

As she closed the boot of the car, Bastian, Gemma and Katherine rounded the corner at the end of their street. Gemma and Katherine took one look at the woman parked outside the house and ran excitedly to greet her. Bastian was bewildered by the girl's behaviour but picked up his speed, too.

"Are you from Starlight Investigations?" Gemma yelled breathlessly.

"Yes, I am," April answered.

"I'm Gemma and this is Katherine."

"I'm sorry," Bastian said catching up, "who are you and what are you doing here?"

"My name is April," she said, instigating a handshake, "and I am a Gatherer attached to the Starlight Investigations Unit."

"The who?"

"We are a group of people who track and capture creatures that are non-indigenous to the Earth and pose a danger to the safety of the human race. I believe you have a vampire across the street that requires relocation."

"Oh, I see," Bastian stated, nodding his head. "You must come in so Gemma can tell you all about it and you can make your assessment. Did the school call you?" he asked, guiding her to the front door.

"No. Gemma rang the call centre who got in touch with me."

"I see. Have you contacted my parents or should I do that now?"

"I think we should hang off contacting your parents until I have gauged the situation and my partner has arrived," April said consulting her watch. "I believe he should be here within the next half an hour or so."

"Your partner?" Bastian stated in a panic. His mind was in turmoil. How had Gemma gotten herself into such a situation? Why couldn't she keep her mouth shut? Bastian would have been able to help her with her delusions if she had given him a chance. Now it seemed that Gemma had alerted the authorities and he believed this woman had come to make a mental health judgement on his sister. Bastian led April to the lounge room, "Make yourself comfortable. Would you like a cup of tea or coffee?"

"No thank you. I would like to get started with Gemma, if you don't mind?"

Bastian did mind. In fact, he minded a lot, but what was he going to say? 'No, you cannot talk to my sister without our parents being present.' He realised there was nothing wrong with him saying just that, so he did.

"You cannot talk to Gemma unless our parents are present. Nothing she tells you can be used in a court of law or a mental health hearing without their initial consent."

"Bastian, I am not here to gauge whether or not your sister's reality functions are intact or not. I already know they are. I am here to gauge how much danger the vampire across the street poses to your family and the best way to capture her and limit the loss of human lives."

"Oh, my God! You really believe she is a vampire. You are just as whacked out as Gemma and her friend there," he said pointing to Katherine.

"Bastian's been bitten by her," Gemma told April as an explanation for his behaviour.

April pulled a gadget out of her handbag, being careful not to hurt Briella or reveal her presence. It looked like a Taser, but where the Taser sent out an electrical shock, this machine sent out a purple light. She put it against his neck and asked Gemma if the placement was right. Gemma tipped her head to indicate the other side. After April adjusted the machine before switching it on. Two fang marks appeared where he had been bitten.

"Wow, look at that!" Katherine exclaimed.

Bastian pulled away from April, "What are you playing at? You shouldn't be encouraging them." He was becoming frightened that this was not some sort of sick joke and that Sarina really was a vampire. His mind hurt. There were no such things as vampires. That was just Sci-Fi/Fantasy rubbish that half the teenage girls and their mothers were into at the moment. Even his girlfriend, Sarah, seemed to be afflicted with this nonsense, asking him to sit through those types of movies with her.

"I'm calling Mum and Dad," he stated petulantly.

"That is not a good idea, Bastian. Adults do not believe these types of creatures exist, which is why you, who are nearly eighteen, are having a hard time believing what is right in front of you. Admittedly, vampires have ways of changing one's perspective," April contemplated aloud, "and with this vamp being female, she has probably got you under her predatory spell."

"What do you mean?" the girls asked intrigued.

VAMPIRE

"The female vampire can somehow make the male human believe she is the most beautiful woman in the world. The male cannot help but be drawn to her perceived beauty which makes it easier for her to catch her meal. Same goes for the male vampire and the female human. She is unable to prevent herself from being drawn to his provocative masculinity."

"What do they really look like?" Gemma asked.

"They are hideous creatures that would curl your toes and make your hair stand on end if you saw them for what they really are. Your blood would run cold and your heart would race so fast with fear it would feel as though it might explode out of your chest," April replied.

All four of them nearly jumped out of their skins when April's phone suddenly shrilled into the silence. Grabbing hold of her chest with her left hand, she pushed the answer button with her right and brought it to her ear.

"Hello, April, it's Sophia, I'm afraid I have some bad news."

"What is it, Soph?" April asked with dread in the pit of her stomach.

"Toranthian's been involved in an accident. The helicopter hit some unseen power lines and he is cut up pretty badly. The medics are currently working on stabilising him but his pilot died at the scene. The Queen has been informed of the situation and is sending a team to transport Toren to Mystique for treatment. He won't be able to return until at least tomorrow night, maybe even Sunday morning. I am so sorry."

"It's not your fault, Sophia, I just hope Toren is going to be okay."

"Of course he is. I don't know why the Queen is sending him to Mystique. He will heal just as quickly on Earth," Sophia said.

"How could he possibly explain his quick recovery to the medical team here? As it is, the Cleaners will have to destroy all blood samples and the results of any other tests they have done on him. With the Queen transferring him, Toren will no longer be their concern. With a bit of luck, he will be out of sight, out of mind. Although if they've already noticed how different he is to humans, I don't think this will hold true."

"Let's hope they transfer him soon then," Sophia stated.

"Do you reckon you could connect me to Rochelle?" April quizzed.

"Sure. I suppose she will want to know what is going on, with them dating and all."

"You know about that?"

"Of course, but we don't go around gossiping and stuff," Sophia said in a huff.

"I'm sorry, Sophia. I didn't mean to imply anything. I was just surprised to hear that you knew about their relationship. We thought if it was common knowledge, they would be reprimanded or worse."

"Well, I can't speak for everybody, especially some of the more emotionally vacant people in the call centre, but there is no way I am spreading hearsay to my superiors, or to speak of such things around those who might think it is their duty to pass on that type of information," Sophia said haughtily. "Give me a couple of minutes to connect the call."

Bastian and the girls were looking at April with concerned eyes. She placed her hand over the mouthpiece and told them her partner had been hurt in an accident and wouldn't be joining them today. She excused herself and walked outside to gain some privacy for her conversation with Rochelle.

Eleven

"Hey, April, are you there?" Rochelle asked breathlessly.

"Thanks, Sophia, talk soon," April said and waited before she heard the line disconnect before continuing. "What's new?" April smacked her forehead with the palm of her hand but didn't have time to dwell on the lame start to the conversation.

"Chasing down a phantasm, April. Kinda busy. Whatcha need?"

"Rochelle, I'm sorry, but I have some bad news for you."

"Okay, what is it?"

"Have you talked to Toren today?"

"No," she said. "Oh damn it; the blasted thing has gone to the ghostly plane."

"Rochelle, this is important. I need your full, undivided attention. Can you do that?"

Rochelle caught the serious tone to her voice and sat on the edge of the bed in the kid's room she was in.

"Okay, April. Sorry, I'm listening."

"Sarina, Queen of the Vampires, has managed to escape Mystique and made her way to Earth. She has been here for at least two nights and has killed at least thirty people. Are you still with me, Love?"

"Yeah, I'm still here. What else?"

"Queen Adair has commanded that Toren takes the lead in her capture as he was the one who managed to relocate her during The

Cleanse. He boarded a helicopter a couple of hours ago to carry out his duties to the Queen. Rochelle, the helicopter crashed, severely injuring him and killing the pilot."

"Where is he, April?"

"The Queen is sending a recovery team to collect him and return him to Mystique."

"You have to intercept them, April. I assume you are on the Gold Coast?"

"I am in the Hinterlands."

"There is no way I will get there in time to stop them from taking him away."

"Rochelle, they are sending him back as soon as he is healed."

"So they say," she growled.

"I don't know what is going on, but the Queen is adamant that Toren hooks up with Sarina here on Earth. I am positive that as soon as he is able to return, she will send him back here to fulfil her wishes."

"What do you think her wishes are?" Rochelle questioned.

"I don't know, Rochelle, but I have the worst feeling in the pit of my stomach. I have never felt this way before and I can't put my finger on the cause of my unease. Rochelle, I think I have lost my trust in the Queen."

April felt so much better after having said what had been on her mind since she had become aware of the arrival of the vampire. She also felt absolutely devastated to have voiced her doubts about the Queen's motives.

"I am sure you haven't done that. Coming up against one of the ancients must be a little unsettling. On top of that, you have been told that someone else is going to take the lead on the Gathering when you are more than capable of handling the issue yourself. Perhaps this has put you a little out of sorts. Hang in there, April. It will probably take a few days for the phantasm to rear its ugly transparent head. If I leave now, I should be able to reach you in a few hours."

"Rochelle, I don't want you to come. If Toren is coming back here to capture this vampire then the last thing he needs is a beautiful distraction like you. Being here will probably end up getting him killed."

"But it's a female vampire," Rochelle spluttered.

"Yes it is, and it is one that Toren has captured before. If he can do it once, he can do it again. Besides, I am here to lend a hand and keep him safe. He will be with you before you know it. I will keep in touch and let you know how things are going, I promise."

"You had better. I want to know the minute he returns."

"I will get him to ring you himself. Good luck with that phantasm. I hope you can convince it the end has come for its time on Earth and that it needs to move on to the next part of its journey."

"Thanks, April. Good luck yourself."

April terminated the call and walked inside the house, gasping in surprise. Briella sat on top of an upside down vase, casually swinging her legs, and chatting vivaciously to her captive audience. "Briella!"

Briella fell off the vase in fright. Her wings flapped furiously, preventing her from face-planting the coffee table. Bastian and the girls, who were kneeling beside the table so they could hear what Briella was saying, fell backwards and landed on their butts. "Please don't be mad," Briella implored, "Bastian wanted to see what else you had in your bag and found me hiding in there."

April was livid to realise she had left her bag behind when she stepped outside. Now she had opened herself up to having to meddle with their minds to remove any memories pertaining to Briella when this was all over.

"Excuse me, April, I think I have done a really stupid thing," Bastian said awkwardly.

"I would have to agree with you there. You should never go into a lady's handbag," she admonished.

"I didn't actually mean that, although I do see your point. Last night, I told Sarina she could come into my bedroom. Is it true that vampires cannot step across the threshold unless invited?"

"I am afraid so," April said placing her hand on his shoulder, "but you can fix this. You just need to rescind your invitation."

"How do I do that?" he asked.

"By stating that you rescind the invitation offered to Sarina."

"Do I have to say it to her?"

"Nope, you just have to say it out loud," April assured him.

"I rescind the invitation to enter my home offered to Sarina the vampire last night," Bastian said, looking around for some sort of indication his incantation had worked. When he didn't receive any, he said, "What did I do wrong?"

"You didn't do anything wrong."

"But nothing happened."

"What did you think would happen?" Gemma asked.

"I don't know. Something to show the magic had worked."

"You are not dealing with magic, Bastian. You are simply rescinding an invitation. You will see tonight that it has worked when Sarina attempts to enter your dwelling and she is unable to step inside," April informed him.

"Yes, except Mum and Dad will be home by then and they will invite her in," he stated.

"Then we will have to make sure they don't," Gemma responded.

"Your Mum would take one look at her and scream with terror. I will make sure your Dad is not inclined to offer an invitation," April said.

"How are you going to do that?" Gemma asked.

"I can be very persuasive," April answered. She didn't go into details about her ability to enter people's minds and plant instructions inside. "I have been told by my superiors that I am not to engage the vampire. When my partner returns, he is to take the lead. I will need to stay with you guys tonight to make sure the vampire returns to Mr. Cameron's after wreaking havoc on the community."

"What makes you think she will do that," Bastian queried.

"She is a vampire, it's what they do."

"She didn't do that last night," Gemma stated.

"Will your parents be home before dark?" April countered, totally ignoring Gemma's statement.

"They should be home in about half an hour," Bastian said looking at his watch.

"We had better get you home, Katherine. It is not safe here."

"Are you kidding? This is the safest house in the country tonight with you here. Please, can I stay?"

"This is not my home. What about your parents?"

"My parents don't go out after dark, and they won't open the door either."

"Really?" asked Gemma. "How come?"

"I don't know, they have always been that way."

"What are their names?" April asked, her curiosity piqued.

"Jill and Braxton Glower." April nodded her head in understanding. "You know them? Did you help them once?"

"Yes, Katherine. I helped them both when they were young like you. I kept my eye on them for years to make sure they were okay. I didn't need to check in so often once they met each other and fell in love. They had somebody to discuss their fears with who would believe them unequivocally. I won't discuss the details with you and you won't bring up painful memories for them by asking them questions about it when you go home. Understood?"

"Understood," Katherine agreed. "So can I stay?"

"Sure," Gemma replied. "I will set it up with my parents. April can you talk Katherine's parents into letting her stay here tonight, please?"

April looked from one to the other. Bastian just sat with a grin on his face. He knew the girls would wear her down, regardless of the fact that this woman apparently dealt with creatures on a regular basis. Bastian got the feeling April didn't cope so well with kids.

"What's their number?"

Katherine gave it to her and then raced upstairs with Gemma to her room where they could make the sleeping arrangements. They pulled out the trundle bed that lived beneath Gemma's bed and retrieved clean linen from the cupboard in the hallway. Briella fluttered from one place to the next with the girls. She had never had a sleepover with anyone other than April.

The Glower's were displeased to hear from April. A call from April meant there was a monster on the loose. They felt a bit better when April stated she was staying the night at Gemma's and they gave the okay for Katherine to have a sleep over. There were only two things left to do. The first was to work out how to get Karen and Walter to allow her to stay the night. The second was to sit tight and not lift a finger to save any of the victims while Sarina went on the killing spree of a lifetime in a rage that Toren was not where she wanted him to be.

Karen and Walter arrived home together. Karen's car had broken down, so Walter had organised for a tow truck to collect the car and take it to the mechanic, while he picked Karen up and brought her home.

They drove the car into the garage and let the automatic door close behind them. After exiting the vehicle, they walked through the door leading to the kitchen. Bastian grabbed the junk mail off the side table and removed the rubber band that held all the pieces of paper in place. He attempted to place April's hair in a ponytail but found himself flat on his back on the floor after she flipped him. He held the rubber band up to show her and asked her to put her hair up. After she complied and lifted him to his feet, he grabbed her hand and led her through the house to meet his parents.

"G'day, son. How was your day?" Walter asked.

"Really good, Dad. I would like you both to meet April," he said pulling her into view. "She is an Olympic athlete from America who has arrived a couple of months ahead of schedule to get in some practice in a warmer climate. Her flights were mixed up and her billeting family are not due to house her until Monday. I was hoping she would be able to stay with us for a few nights until her Australian family are able to meet their obligations."

"Well, this is all a bit sudden, don't you think?" Karen asked. The fact that her son was holding hands with this tall, attractive young woman hadn't escaped her notice.

"April can have my room. I'll take the couch downstairs," Bastian said.

"Well, actually," April said putting on an authentic sounding accent, "I am not accustomed to your time zone and won't get any sleep at night until I acclimatise. I would be more than happy to stay down here on the couch if it is okay to stay for a couple of days."

"I would be horrified to think of Bastian representing Australia in another country and finding himself stranded with no-one willing to give him any hospitality," Walter said. "Of course you can stay. Where is your stuff?"

"In my rental car," April said, surprised by how easy that was. "Thank you for opening your home to me. Can I help with dinner?"

"Of course not, you are a guest in my home. What is your speciality?" Karen asked.

"I beg your pardon?"

"What sport are you competing in?"

"Oh, swimming."

"I'm sorry, young lady, but you've got no chance against our Aussie swimmers," Walter stated.

"Walt!" Karen said with a raised voice. "That was rude!"

"Well, it's the truth, isn't it?"

"That's beside the point," Karen told him, smacking his chest.

"Hi, Mum," Gemma said as she bounded into the room. "Katherine is going to stay the night, okay? I'll give you a hand preparing dinner. Out all of you," she commanded, flapping her arms. "We've got some work to do. Oh, is April staying too?"

"You know April?" Karen and Walter asked.

"Sure," Bastian answered, "Principal Jackson introduced April to the cohort at assembly this afternoon."

"Go on, get out all of you. Katherine, you can stay and chat with me while I help Mum if you like."

"Can I hang in your room for a little while? I am feeling a bit tired," Katherine queried.

"Yeah, sure. The bed's ready for you and dinner will be about an hour," Gemma said, knowing Katherine really wanted to get back to Briella.

Walter, Bastian and April moved into the lounge room where Walter turned on the television to watch the early news. Bastian and April sat at the breakfast nook in the corner and thought they would have to talk about the Olympic Games. They soon discovered that

Walter was quite absorbed in the news and when the ads came on, he simply flicked the channel until he found something else that grabbed his attention. Bastian was still coming to grips with the idea that monsters were real and spent most of their time together quizzing her about her job. Karen and Gemma began preparing dinner while Katherine asked Briella lots of questions about fairies.

April remained relaxed and enjoyed Bastian's company right up until the minute the sun dipped below the horizon and their meal was placed on the dining room table. April knew that the human toll was going to be huge and she was unable to do anything about it.

Twelve

Sarina's eyes flew open as the sun went to bed for the night. She got up and peered through the bedroom window. The people living in the house out back were sitting down to their evening meal. Something Sarina was really looking forward to. With any luck, this would be her last night on Earth and she hoped her favourite blood types would be readily available for her to savour.

It would be extremely fortuitous to come across another group of people that held the same DNA as the woman and her three children from two nights ago. That meal had been a few levels above delicious.

Sarina made her way to the front of the house and her eyes blazed with anger. Across the road, she saw Karen and Walter seated at the ends of the table. On one long side sat Gemma and her friend and on the other sat Bastian and the Gatherer. "How dare she insinuate herself into their lives!" she fumed into the darkness.

Then she began to wonder what this meant for her reunion with Toranthian and her anger escalated further. Perhaps this Gatherer had not taken her demand that he be there seriously. Should that be the case, she decided she would double her earlier estimate and kill at least two thousand humans before the next sunrise.

Sarina went back to the bedroom and raided the closet. She wasn't sure whether she wanted to dress as provocative siren or as a murderess. Somewhere in the middle she decided, grabbing a pair of full-length black pants that were very flattering to her figure. She paired that with a thin strapped, low cut, red satin shirt and a short sleeved, black, fitted jacket. A pair of black stilettos finished the outfit but would have to be carried to the meeting place as the heels would not last a couple of minutes with the speeds she was capable of travelling.

Sarina was certainly in no mood for a quiet stroll and she wasn't entirely sure the heels would hold up over the distance if she were to walk at a human's pace. She figured this type of footwear was utterly useless for anything other than improving the shape of the leg and butt of the wearer and gaining the interest of the male of the species.

Sarina made her way to the front door, glaring at April through the window. She wondered why she wasn't preparing to leave. It would take her a lot longer to get to the clearing than it would Sarina. *'Maybe April has no intention of* attending. *Perhaps Toren has been given the sole task of capturing her and April has been taken off the case. That would be perfect,'* she thought.

It was time to get something to eat. Sarina opened the door and exited the building. April and Sarina's eyes locked together and in that moment, Sarina learned her earlier thought had been correct. April had been told to stand down. Sarina could see the lines of anger, frustration, and helplessness imprinted all over her face. Sarina smiled and tipped her hand as a salute. April's eyes narrowed in response.

April thought about the message she had received regarding Toren's accident and his transfer to Mystique for treatment. Sarina growled in frustration but then threw her head back with laughter at the devastation she was going to cause. In the blink of an eye, she was gone into the night. April attempted to re-join the conversation at the table but her mind kept wandering. It was going to be a very long night.

"Are you all right, April?" Karen asked. "You seem so far away."

"Oh, I'm sorry for being so rude," April replied. "I was thinking about my family."

"How many people in your family?" Walter asked.

"Just Mom, Dad and me," April replied, keeping it simple.

"Is this your first time away from home?" Karen asked.

"No, but it is the first time away from my country," April stated.

"What do your parents do for a living?" Walter questioned.

"You're not helping," Bastian said. "Have you finished your dinner, April? Then let's go and watch some television. That will get your mind off things for a little while. Tomorrow, I will show you around the neighbourhood."

April and Bastian left the table and moved to the living room, while the girls cleared the table and the adults washed the dishes and put them away. April chose to sit on the left-hand cushion of the three seater lounge and Bastian sat beside her in the middle. He positioned himself so he could see her face and the television with ease.

She was just as beautiful as Sarina, except April's beauty was real whereas Sarina's was a mere projection. Her long blonde hair with caramel highlights allowed her to hide her face from prying eyes. With her hair placed in a ponytail, he was able to admire her features.

April had the bluest eyes he had ever seen. They were the same colour as the shirt, pants and boots she wore. Her cheekbones were nicely defined and her lips were small and plump. She had long eyelashes and thin, neat eyebrows. Her neck was long and slender and she had an athletic body that was still feminine in all the right places.

Bastian leaned forward and released her hair from the elastic band. April didn't attempt to stop him but was ready to defend herself from his advances if the need arose. "These things are no good for your hair," he reminded her.

"They tend to split the end of the hair and it is nearly impossible to repair the damage. I would hate for you to have to cut it."

"How do you know about bands and women's hair?"

"My friend, Sarah, tells me about this sort of stuff all the time."

"Have you been dating long?"

"We are not dating," Bastian said.

April looked at him as though she wasn't born yesterday.

"Okay, we are kind of dating. We see each other a couple of nights a week," he admitted. "We are open to seeing other people."

"Does Sarah know that?" April queried.

"Yes," Bastian lied.

"We are not going to start seeing each other, Bastian."

"Why not? We are both consenting adults."

"No, we are not. You are under eighteen and I am a lot older than that," she stated. "You need to be with people closer to your own age."

"What's a few years," Bastian said, placing his hand on her leg.

"Try a few thousand," April informed him.

Bastian looked crushed. "You don't need to lie to convince me to stop hitting on you, April. You just had to say I'm not your type."

April picked up the letter opener sitting on the coffee table. She used it to slice the skin on her arm open and then hovered her other hand over the top. A white light appeared and then faded away. Bastian looked at her skin to see the cut had healed completely, without a scar. He grabbed a tissue from the sideboard and cleaned up her arm.

"What are you?" he asked her, preferring to stand.

"I am a Gatherer."

"What else? Are you even human?"

"Yes and no. I was born on Earth and lived here for twenty-one years. I was then transferred to another planet where I went through an evolutionary process by being exposed to high levels of radiation. I am able to heal myself, among other things, and am three thousand and twenty-one years old."

"Why do you chase monsters?"

"It is my job. It is what I was destined to do."

"You make it sound as though you were manufactured in a lab."

"I kind of was. Bastian, everyone I knew on Earth is dead. Every human I meet will die sooner or later, and yet I will continue on."

"You are immortal?"

"Yes, it seems so."

"Cool."

April let that statement slide. He was a teenager who had not fully understood the ramification of her words. She hoped he never did. As a victim of Sarina's, his memories will not be tampered with as was stated in their rules. However, the knowledge of Briella will be taken away and he will be sworn to secrecy to never speak of April's gifts with an adult.

"So, vampires are real?" Bastian questioned.

"Yes, they are."

"And they are nothing like the vampires portrayed in the movies?"

"No, they are dangerous predators that care nothing for humans or each other. Vampires live in a hierarchy and follow the instructions given by their maker. Their only pleasure lies in killing their prey."

"Where do they come from?"

"We don't know where they originally came from. They arrived on Earth through a wormhole in our solar system. It took us six months to remove them all from the planet."

"How many were there?"

"One thousand and twenty-three, including Sarina. She is their Queen."

"How did she get back here and why is she here?"

"I don't know," April lied. She didn't want to tell him about the portals that were situated on Earth. She thought it would be better if Bastian thought this was a rare incident with only a slight possibility of something like this happening again. "When my partner is well enough, he will come and help me take care of her."

"Are you going to kill her?"

"Not exactly. Bastian, you really don't need to concern yourself with this. She will not hurt you or any members of your family. I won't let that happen."

"What about everybody else? It's night time. Where is she and what is she doing?"

April didn't answer. Her eyes moved to the window but they weren't focussed on the view. Her mind was wondering where Sarina was going to go now that she knew Toren was not going to appear. She was very disappointed that her Queen had refused to allow her to capture the vampire on her own. Yes, Toren had caught her last time, but she had been given the same training as him in the art of capturing creatures and she was just as capable as him. Probably even more so, due to her being female.

When April didn't answer him, Bastian said, "She is going to kill people, isn't she?"

This time, she answered, "Yes, she is and I am not allowed to do a damned thing to stop it!"

Thirteen

Sarina came across five people on the way to the park. She didn't play with her food, just took what she needed in preparation for her killing spree. Sarina was in two minds by the time she reached the park. She hoped Toren would be there so she could make their union complete.

She missed having Karayan around to help her rule her children. Now that he was immersed in the eternal death, she needed Toren to complete her needs. Yet the moment that she turned him and the process of becoming a vampire had begun, she would be required to leave this planet and return to imprisonment.

Sarina enjoyed the process of hunting her food. She loved being able to choose whom she drank from. She loved the tightness and the freshness of the packaging that came with the food on Earth. *'Who knows how long it will take to organise a revolution on Mystique?'* she thought.

The possibility of the many creatures imprisoned on Mystique working together to achieve the goal of acquiring access to the portal and escaping was slim at best. It would be quite a while before she was able to return to Earth and it would be nice to spend a little more time learning how the planet had changed.

Sarina couldn't afford to become complacent, however. She had informed April of the consequences that would occur if her demands remained unfulfilled and she had to keep her promise or lose her fear factor. Climbing to the top of the monkey bars and sitting with her legs hanging over the edge, she decided to wait for a couple of hours to see what happened. She wouldn't take any more lives unless forced to. There was no point in having the liquid in her stomach sloshing around when she travelled to her next destination.

The moon hung low in the sky and cast very little light on the area. It would have been a very romantic setting for a date with her partner, had she been human. Still, the setting for coming face to face with Toranthian after so many years seemed to be important to her. She wondered if he had aged in the time she had been away. Had his gifts kept him young or would she find him looking old and ragged.

April, the other Gatherer was youthful in appearance. Surely Toranthian would have aged at the same rate as her and would still look as youthful as he did in his heydey. Sarina's mouth began watering just thinking about how handsome he had been. It wasn't just his physical packaging that had caught her eye. His persona had a lot to do with her attraction to him.

Toranthian was one hundred and eighty centimetres tall with a weight builder's physique. His hair was dark and his eyes were grey. He had a strong chin with a muscle that twitched along his left jawline. The last time they had been together, he had placed a mask laced with silver over her mouth to prevent her from biting him. Her hands and feet were tied together with silver netting and he had thrown her over his shoulder like she was a sack of potatoes. She looked forward to him throwing her around again and showing off his strength.

The park was quiet for a Friday night. There was not a soul in sight. Perhaps there had been a warning for people to stay away. Sarina had ignored the yellow tape that surrounded the boundaries not realising it had been placed there by the Starlight team to keep people out.

Under normal circumstances, the tape would have been placed there by police wanting to seal off the area so they could collect their forensic evidence. It seemed that word had gotten around and the people had decided to stay away and not come for a gawk.

Sarina waited patiently. She had all the time in the world to spend with her intended. It was easy for her to be still for a couple of hours. A human may have found it boring and begun fidgeting. She listened to the wildlife in the area and found there were many sounds she didn't recognise and some that she expected to hear that were not evident. It seemed that a lot more than the landscape had changed in her absence.

Once the two hours had passed, Sarina jumped down from the monkey bars and headed towards the Convention and Exhibition Centre. She arrived towards the end of the show and grabbed the handles of the doors and bent them so they were twisted together, locking the audience inside. She entered the remaining doors and twisted the handle from the inside, effectively blocking all exits.

The skaters were twirling and dancing on the ice with their audience completely captivated by their skill. Sarina watched them herself, intrigued by the way their bodies glided on the ice with such ease and grace.

She had never considered humans to be graceful creatures. She had always thought of them as clumsy and inadequate. What she saw before her was quite beautiful. Sarina sat and watched the end of the show. When it had finished, she rose with the rest of the audience as they applauded the troupe.

The claw on her pointer finger extended and she began slicing the throats of the humans closest to her. This time, she chose to skip over the children and had decided to let the skaters live too. Screams began filling the centre and those closest to the doors suddenly found themselves being crushed against them as they refused to open.

Sarina wasn't sure how many she ended up killing but knew it would get the message across. Toranthian would present himself to her, or she would continue to hurt people until he did. Sarina sat down to wait for the authorities to show. She would kill those as well before finding a new place to stay for the day.

Now that the Gatherer had made herself cosy at Bastian's place, she would not be able to return to Carl's. She would find herself captured during the daylight hours when she was not at her full strength. That was the only thing she loved about Mystique. For all but a couple of hours every two centuries, their land lay in complete darkness. Her children were only forced into a death-like sleep during daylight hours.

April and Bastian were discussing the changes that humans had undergone since The Cleanse and how they had forgotten the existence of the monsters that used to torment their ancestors. She indicated how, in the previous thirty years, books and movies had gone from the creatures being at the centre of a horror story to a romance, with the creature being the hero.

Bastian was trying to understand how something so awful could be so easily forgotten.

"How often do you think about the black plague or the holocaust?" she asked him.

"I don't," he answered.

"So how do you expect your species to remember things that hunted your ancestors, thousands of years ago?"

A fluttering of wings ended their conversation.

"Hi, April, the girls are still awake. Katherine is about to tell Gemma about her brush with a Bogeyman. I know you don't want to know this, but Sarina has begun her killing spree."

"How do you know that?" Bastian asked.

"I am a Locator Fairy. I know these things," Briella answered.

April's phone began to vibrate. She had turned the ringtone to silent when the girls had settled down for the night and the parents had retired to the upper floor.

"Hello."

"Hi, April, it's Sophia. How are you doing?"

"Fine, how bad is it?"

"We have picked up multiple triple zero calls from the Gold Coast Convention and Exhibition Centre. It appears there has been a major incident. We are sending two teams to take care of the survivors and the deceased."

"Do you want us to track her?"

"No, your orders remain the same. I am sorry, April."

"Thanks, Sophia," April said as she terminated the call. "I wish I could go for a run, I need something physical to do."

"I can help you with that," Bastian said pushing her back into the seat and kissing her tenderly. "No strings attached," he whispered.

Briella didn't wait around to see him get hurt. She flew quickly up the stairs to listen to Katherine's story about the Bogeyman.

Fourteen

Gemma and Katherine sat on the trundle bed, which was hidden from the doorway by Gemma's bed. The girls had turned the bedroom light off but had switched Gemma's bedside lamp on. It cast a soft golden glow in the room, chasing away the shadows. Katherine wasn't sure where to start or how much of the experience she even wanted to tell Gemma.

What she did know was Gemma would want to know it all. Perhaps April would wipe Gemma's memories anyway, but it was a very scary, personal experience and she didn't want anything to be awkward between them afterwards if that turned out to be not the case.

Gemma could tell that Katherine was feeling a bit unsure about opening up. "You don't have to tell me what happened if you don't want to. After discovering Sarina is a vampire and that monsters truly exist, well I can understand the trepidation you must be feeling. Besides, I can only imagine the kinds of thoughts you must be suppressing," Gemma frowned.

"No, it's okay, Gemma. You have no idea how hard it has been to live with this for so long and not be able to discuss it with anyone."

"How long ago did this happen?"

"Three years."

"Tommy won't talk about it and being only three years old when it happened, Mum and Dad have pretty well convinced him there are no monsters under the bed, just bad dreams that scare little boys. They put a night light on for him when they tuck him in and he is asleep within minutes of his head hitting the pillow," Katherine grimaced.

"How long does it take you to get to sleep?"

"Quite a bit longer than a couple of minutes. A light isn't going to keep the monsters away, is it?"

"No, it's not. So how do you manage to fall asleep?"

"I tell myself that Callum and his friends are out there protecting us from the likes of them. I also believe that a person couldn't possibly be targeted more than once in a lifetime, especially with the overabundance of people living on the planet. That helps to calm my fears when the lights go out and I am on my own. As you saw in the library, help is only a speed dial away. If I got into any trouble, I could dial their number and even if I didn't get a chance to talk, they could trace the call and find me."

"What if you don't get a chance to dial their number?" Gemma queried.

"I didn't call Callum for help. I didn't even know he existed and yet like a knight in shining armour, he was there to protect Tommy and me from that hideous thing."

"What did it look like?"

"It was ghastly. It was human-like, but not, at the same time. Its skin was mottled grey and its teeth were pointed like those of a great white shark. Oh my God, Gemma, its breath stank like rotting fish."

"Where did it come from?"

"My wardrobe. I was just about to drift off to sleep, when the doors to my wardrobe flew open. The banging of the doors against my wall had me scrambling into a sitting position, with the blankets tucked protectively beneath my chin, but then I noticed this swirling blue light inside my closet. The light was so pretty, Gemma. It was calming, almost mesmerising, and I could feel myself beginning to relax. After a while, which was probably no more than a minute, I found myself throwing the covers back and my feet sinking into the plush carpet. I took a couple of steps forward and then this thing, the Bogeyman Callum called it, stepped out of the swirling gateway, and I froze. I should have screamed, or run out of the room, but I did neither of those things. I just stood there, like an idiot, waiting for the thing to grab me."

"Did it grab you, Katherine?" Gemma placed her hand on Katherine's arm.

"Yes," she whispered, as tears rolled down her face. "It strode over to me, wrapped its clawed hands around my arms and peered into my face with its stinky breath. The smell made me feel so sick, I threw up all over myself and I was so scared, I peed my pants."

Gemma took both of Katherine's hands in her own and gently rubbed them with her thumbs. "I would have been terrified too, and reacted the same way."

"Really?" Katherine asked.

"Damn straight, girl. Look at the goose bumps that have sprouted all over my arms, and I haven't even come face to face with the damned thing. I am surprised you can even manage to talk about it with me. I feel like wetting my pants, I am so scared. I never imagined anything like this could be real. I thought that parents just made up stories like these to scare themselves and their kids around campfires. Holy crap, I am never going to be able to get to sleep again."

"Of course you will, Gemma. You slept like a baby last night with Sarina across the street."

"Yes, but I thought she wouldn't be able to get out of the house with crosses and garlic all over the place. I was wrong. This thing that came after you, it came out of your cupboard, for goodness sake. What else is out there, Katherine? Does every creature that people have ever thought up to put in storybooks and movies actually exist?"

"I don't know. I asked Callum that very question. He told me not to worry my pretty little head about such things. He said he would be keeping an eye on Tommy and me, and then promised nothing would ever hurt us again."

"How did Callum protect you? Did he burst into your bedroom?"

"No, he set a trap and allowed himself to be captured by the creature so he could find us."

"Where were you?"

"The Bogeyman had taken us back to its dimension, before Callum knew of its existence."

"What do you mean?"

"Tommy and I were the first people targeted. Thanks to Callum, we were also the last." Katherine pulled her hands out of Gemma's, got off the bed and walked to the window. It was quiet outside. The leaves on the trees were calm, a striking contrast to the turmoil that was currently going on inside of Katherine.

"What was the other dimension like?"

"It was cold, dark and wet. The walls were slimy and the floor was slippery. I couldn't see my hands in front of me, but I could hear Tommy sobbing. I tried to follow the sound but it took me a long time to find him. It was really hard to pinpoint where his voice originated from, so I basically kept walking backwards and forwards until I tripped over him. I gave him such a fright, even though I was talking to him. His screams nearly burst my eardrums. It was lucky Callum found us when he did. I don't know how much longer I could have survived."

"What did he do to you?"

"By the time Callum found us, I had lost my right kidney, my appendix, my right lung, and the glands in my right armpit."

"Oh my God!" Gemma groaned.

"Tommy had both his eyes removed, and his tongue."

"How is that even possible?"

"I don't know how we survived him tearing out our body parts."

"But you can play sport and everything. How do you not get short of breath?"

"Callum healed us," Katherine shrugged. She turned around to face Gemma. "I can see why Callum and his team modify memories and are careful to ensure adults do not become privy of their abilities. Imagine the demand in the medical field alone for their services. I do not have one scar on my body to show the trauma I have been through, neither does Tommy. As you know, Tommy has both eyes and his tongue. If they did a scan on my body they would see everything in its right place.

"Callum was not allowed to heal the emotional scars, which will stay with me forever. With a bit of luck, they will lessen in intensity over time. Even after three years, I can remember the pain from him ripping my skin open to get to the pieces that he wanted. I will never forget the shriek of Tommy's terror and pain, as his eyes were scooped out like melons and then the moist, gurgling sound in his throat as his tongue was removed."

"Did Callum kill it?"

"No. They are forbidden to kill the creatures they hunt."

"How could they not? Wouldn't you feel better with it dead?"

"Yes, I would. I cannot deny that I wish the creature was dead. Yet, I get upset when I see on television that somebody has been bitten by a shark and then all these people are calling for it to be found and killed. The shark is just doing what feels natural to it at the time. I guess if we are food for this creature, I shouldn't be upset because it wanted something to eat."

"This is completely different, Katherine."

"Why is it? They are both predatory animals. One living in the ocean, one living on the land."

"Yes, but one is indigenous to the Earth and the other is clearly not."

"You don't know that the Bogeymen were not here first. Callum told me that the Earth had been purged of predatory animals to give the humans a chance to become what nature intended. How do you know that we were here before those creatures and that they are the ones who are alien to our planet? For all we know, we might be the ones who have come to Earth from another planet. The scientists living today are searching for a planet capable of sustaining human life. As if destroying one planet isn't enough. Who's to say we haven't already destroyed many planets with our greed and feelings of grandeur.

"I hope to never come across a creature that wished to do humans harm again in my lifetime. I am eternally grateful there are people like Callum and April placed on this planet, who watch for these types of creatures and are more than capable of dealing with them. In some ways, I am also pleased to discover they are not killed outright. This gives me hope that we, as humans, will learn to value life, no matter what form it comes in, or what danger it poses to us or our way of life."

Gemma didn't think she agreed with Katherine's philosophy. She would have wanted the creature to be dead, just as she wants Sarina to be dead. How could her brother possibly be safe with that creature still out there? She realised, however, that Katherine had been living with these horrific memories for the past three years and had thought about what she would have hoped the outcome to have been on many occasions.

Perhaps, when Gemma had been given three years to consider her own circumstances, fears, and desires, she would come up with a different philosophy than the one she held at the moment. So as not to say anything that might damage their relationship, Gemma asked, "What does Callum look like? Is he hot or what?"

"What," Katherine replied, giggling alongside Gemma. "No, seriously, he is not that bad looking, but he certainly wouldn't make the top ten list of Hunky Dories. The thing with Callum is, his personality sucks you in and makes him appear more attractive than he really is. He's got shaggy brown hair at the front, but it's short at the back. Brown eyes, chiselled chin, nice lips, tall weedy body. He likes to wear black leather pants but doesn't really have any butt or leg muscles to fill them out. He likes to stand like a girl with his hand on his hip and the other tucked under his chin, like he is in deep thought. Callum calls this his 'playing it cool look'."

"And what do you call it?" Gemma asked with a smile.

"His feminine stance."

Gemma snorted with laughter, sending Katherine into another fit of giggles.

"Go to sleep, you two!" Karen yelled, from the comfort of her bed.

"Yes, Mother," Gemma chuckled.

"I asked him what he would say to the Bogeyman if he ever saw him again, and he lifted his middle finger and said, 'Suck it'."

"It's a pity I will never get the chance to meet him."

"Yeah, he's funny as, Gemma."

"Perhaps you could have a sixteenth birthday party and invite him," Gemma suggested.

"That's a great idea. I wonder if he would come."

"Have you seen him since he saved you?"

"Yeah, but always from a distance. He has kept his word about keeping an eye on us. He doesn't seem too keen on being friends, though."

"You don't know that for sure. It would look kind of odd, if he struck up a friendship with you. You are still a bit young, considering other people would see him to be a stranger, I mean."

"I guess you are right, Gemma. Anyway, I am getting a bit tired. Do you think we could go to sleep now?"

"Sure. Do you feel safe enough to fall asleep?"

"Are you kidding? Like I said to April earlier, this is the safest house in the country tonight."

Gemma got up off the trundle bed and jumped into her own. "Good night, Katherine. Sweet dreams."

"Same to you," Katherine responded, climbing into her bed for the night.

Fifteen

In the morning, Gemma and Katherine bounded downstairs. April was sitting on the chaise facing the window with her head back and her eyes closed. Gemma peered into her face and jumped in surprise when April opened her eyes.

"Oh, I thought you were asleep. Sorry to wake you, April."

"You didn't, Gemma, I was just resting my eyes."

"Did the vampire come back?"

"Nope."

"Is she dead then?"

"No. She will have found somewhere else to stay. She spotted me here last night and wouldn't risk me removing her while she was sleeping."

"So Bastian isn't in any danger now?"

"I wouldn't go that far, Gemma. She has tasted him and let him live. His blood answers to her now. There must be a reason he is still walking around. You need to watch yourself. Sarina wouldn't have taken too kindly to you putting stuff up all over her house, even if it was to protect your brother. I wouldn't be surprised if she didn't come for you some time, too."

Katherine stood there nodding her head in agreement. "You will stay and take care of them, won't you, April?"

"I will be here until my friend is well. Once he is capable of carrying out his duties, I will be leaving to assist him to take this vampire down."

"You must be tired. Do you want to lie down on my bed for a sleep?" Gemma asked.

'No thanks. I got a couple of hours last night. That will keep me going. I might nap for an hour this afternoon before the sun sets."

"What do you want to do today then, April?" Katherine asked.

"I need to get to the gym and do some training. Some swimming would be good, too. Do you want to come with me, if it's okay with Karen and Walter?"

"You bet," the girls chorused.

Karen and Walter were thrilled to have the girls taken care of for the morning. It saved them worrying about the teenagers wandering the streets. Having April stay for a couple of days was a great decision. The girls had somebody interesting to spend time with and the opportunity to learn a bit about Americans and their cultural perspectives.

Briella chose to stay at home in Gemma's room. She flew to the top of the wardrobe, and decided to spend the morning chilling out, after April gave her a chunk of mushroom for breakfast.

The girls enjoyed a leisurely swim at the local pool and caught up with a few friends from school. They hired some inflatable pool toys to sit on and held races up and down the lanes.

Once April had completed her weights training, she too hit the pool. The girls decided to give her a race but were left for dead. They had no trouble believing she was there to train for the Olympic Games. She was a fish in the water and her style was effortless and smooth. Once she had completed twenty laps, the girls offered her one of their inflatables for a bit of fun and frivolity.

April declined their offer, but the girls persisted in pestering her until she gave in. She found that it was quite enjoyable trying to balance on top of the toy while attempting to push her opponent off theirs. For the first time ever, April gained an understanding as to why her friend Force preferred to work with the kids who were being targeted by the creatures, rather than the adults. She was actually having fun and exercising at the same time.

The girl's tummies began to growl and they asked April if they could head home for some lunch. April helped them pack up and returned the inflatable toys to the service desk. On their way to the car, they spotted Bastian and Sarah walking hand in hand, with Max on a lead.

"Hey, Sarah," Gemma called.

"Hi, Gemma, how are you?" she answered.

"Great. See you later," Gemma waved.

Bastian avoided looking at April. He kept his eyes focussed on the top of Max's head, who was now busily slobbering all over April's hand. After Bastian had kissed April the previous night and she had moved her knee to make its acquaintance with his groin, he went upstairs to bed, and had discovered she'd left the house when he came downstairs in the morning.

"Hello, I'm Sarah."

"April."

"Come on, April, we're starving," Katherine called.

The girls piled in the car while April placed their bags in the boot. She smirked as Bastian tried to assure Sarah that April was nobody important and he didn't have any interest in her whatsoever. Once April had gotten behind the wheel and started the engine, Gemma asked her what her plans for the rest of the day were.

April wasn't sure. She would check with Briella to see if she had picked up any other creatures on her radar. If she had, then she would begin tracking the creature and working on a plan for taking care of it. If not, she would have to find another way to keep herself busy.

They arrived home and headed for the kitchen.

Gemma told April where to find the plates while she got the bread out of the bread bin and the peanut butter out of the cupboard. Katherine retrieved the strawberry jam and orange juice from the fridge.

"What are we eating?" April asked.

"Peanut butter and jam sandwiches."

"Do you mean peanut butter and jelly?" April enquired, as Karen appeared through the doorway.

"Hello there, girls. Did you enjoy your swim?"

"We sure did," Gemma stated. "Can't you see our glowing faces?"

"Well, yes I can," Karen answered. "Thank you for taking them with you this morning, April. I hope they weren't any trouble."

"No, of course not. Actually, we had a lot of fun."

"What are your plans for this afternoon? Did you get any sleep last night?"

"I got a little bit. I might have a lie down if that is okay with you?" April said, wanting to appear completely human. "I am feeling a bit tired. Gemma said earlier that I could lie down on her bed."

"Sure. Go up the stairs and it's the second door on your right," Karen replied.

April consumed the sandwich and glass of juice then headed upstairs. She lay down on the bed and fell asleep through sheer boredom. Her phone vibrating in her pocket woke her an hour later.

"Hi, April, it's Force. How are you going?"

"Good, Liam, how are you?"

"I'm good. Are you busy?"

"Not at the moment, what's up?"

"I've got a little situation down here. Scout and I are tracking a couple of creatures and I think I am going to need some backup. They have taken six children, which we believe are still alive, and I could use some assistance to help them recover from their ordeal."

"What sort of monsters are you chasing?"

Force laughed, "You sound like Scout. That's what she calls them. Anyhoo, Scout and I think they are a new breed, created by the imaginations of the children themselves."

"What sort of monster could be created by children?"

"Jealousy monsters. It is a very volatile emotion and we believe these monsters have somehow manifested themselves through the power of the children's jealousy."

"Wow, I would love to investigate this further. I can come down now, but have to be back before dark. Do you think that would be a problem?"

"No, if I can't get this done before dark, you are more than welcome to leave. I can handle it on my own, just thought it would be quicker and better for the kids if I had some help."

"What cover do you want me to use?"

"Federal Agent."

After April got his location, she and Briella headed off. She told Karen she had been contacted by a distant cousin who had just been informed of her arrival and had asked her to come for the afternoon. April asked if it was still okay for her to come back and stay the night. Karen was more than happy to accommodate April as Gemma seemed to be very taken with her.

April jumped in the car and put the pedal to the metal. She was looking forward to catching up with Liam and doing some Gatherer work.

"Do you think Scout will be there?" Briella asked excitedly.

"I know she is there," April responded.

"Oh goodie," Briella said, clapping her hands while hovering near April's ear. "Can I spend some time with her?"

"Sure you can. It sounds like her job is done and Liam's has just begun."

It took an hour to drive to his location. Once she got there, she was unable to contact him. She asked Briella if she knew where Scout was, but Briella couldn't locate her either. They drove into the main part of town and found a group of people gathering in the grounds of the local church. April showed his picture around and asked if any of the patrons knew him.

"Yes, we know him. He is a private investigator looking into the disappearances of the children in the district" replied Mrs.

Landscombe, one of the fundraising committee members.

"My name is April, I am a federal agent assisting with the investigation. Can you tell me where I can find Private Investigator Force?"

"He's probably at Loretta's place. Her daughter has run away."

"Where will I find her?"

Mrs. Landscombe gave April directions to Loretta's place. As April pulled into the driveway, she felt Force connect with her mind. She discovered he had found the children and was sending them down the hillside on their own. He had to help a couple of children who were still being held by the creatures. Force gave her a little background information on the children and told her where she could locate them. April changed direction and drove the car through the paddock and over the hill. There she saw six children huddling together in the distance.

April called for the Cleaners and began the task of modifying the memories of the children.

It was their law that the children be allowed to remember their ordeal but to tone down the feelings associated with the memory to the point where their mind didn't disassociate itself from reality. These children would always remember that monsters existed, but were encouraged to never talk about their tribulations with the creatures, to adults. When telling their story, the perpetrator was to always be construed as human. Otherwise, the adults would send them for professional psychological help which could tie a child's life up for years on the couch.

April finished with the children in an hour at which time the Cleaners had arrived to take them to their special facilities for the night to ensure the memory modification process had been effective. As they had been helped by six local children, April then began working on their memories. She removed any memories they had of Scout. Next, she took away any knowledge they had of Force's special abilities. She then implanted new memories into their minds with a believable scenario that would explain their part in the capture of the two teenagers who had kidnapped the local children.

April then took it upon herself to attempt to place a cautionary note into their personalities. What they had done was dangerous and she hoped that if they were to come across another dangerous situation, they would think twice about jumping in, rather than contacting the authorities. This last implant was not as likely to take as her previous ones. It was very hard to change the basic characteristics of a person, and each of these children was inherently brave.

Once she was finished, the Cleaners took them to their facility as well but only for a couple of hours, before allowing the children to go back home to their parents. April made her way back to Loretta's place where she knew Force to be.

April arrived to discover that once again Force had gotten himself into trouble with the ladies. Being extremely good-looking, sporting a buzz cut, beautiful dark brown eyes and muscles to die for, highlighted by a black singlet and tight black pants, it was no wonder women found him irresistible. Force heard her arrive and went to meet her so he could explain quietly that he would be introducing her as his sister-in-law.

He had pretended to be married when Loretta showed her strong attraction for him by inviting him to dinner when he was in the guise of Dr. Wade Force. When he was pretending to be a Private Investigator, she kissed him, and he didn't have the heart to tell her a second time that he was married, considering his response to her kiss. April noticed the way Force's pulse increased when he talked about her.

She placed her arm through his and stepped forward to meet the woman who might have finally stolen Liam's heart. Loretta was tall and very attractive in her pale blue shirt, dark blue jeans and brown ankle boots. Loretta's chestnut coloured hair was pulled back into a ponytail and her eyes lit up like a Christmas tree when she spotted him. April could tell by the way he spoke to her that he actually liked the woman.

Next, she was introduced to Calamity, Loretta's daughter, who had been encouraged by the Jealousy Monsters to run away with them. She was twelve years old and had auburn hair and green eyes. She wore a red and black shirt with blue jeans and black and white sneakers. She had a different kind of beauty to her mother and would grow up to be striking in her own right.

Michelle and Paul stepped forward to shake hands with April. They were real estate agents in navy coloured business suits and parents to Jacinta, a spunky little blonde with blue eyes, pink outfit and a miniature version of her mother. April had picked up on the potential for Jacinta to become a Battle Star when she had told April in no uncertain terms, that luck had nothing to do with the events that had transpired that afternoon in locating the missing children.

"Has that been taken care of?" April asked Force quietly.

"Guardian Karah will be putting things in place, shortly," he responded.

Force walked over to the railing so that Scout could leave his pocket and join Briella who was hiding beneath the house. April joined him and mentioned how lovely it would be to have a home in the country. Michelle and Paul, upon hearing her comment, immediately began trying to convince April to purchase the property down the road with her non-existent husband, and making this town her base when she wasn't working a case. Believing that Force was her brother-in-law, they included him in the conversation of buying the property as a family deal. April had never considered living in the country before. It seemed a lot of things were changing for her this week.

It was a pretty place and the people she had met seemed to be lovely, on the surface. The children were a lot nicer than their city cousins, and it was actually refreshing to see so much of nature and so little of modern construction. April wanted some time to consider the pros and cons of living in the country. That was not going to happen with the adults on the deck excitedly encouraging her to say yes right away.

April thanked them all for their warm welcome and hospitality. She expressed her regret at having to leave with Force to tie up some loose ends in the kidnapping case. What she really wanted was to discuss the possibilities of purchasing the property together with Force.

They walked down the stairs and headed towards the vehicle. Jacinta asked that they return to say goodbye before leaving town altogether. Force agreed and noticed the adults had come to wave them off, too. It was getting late in the afternoon and Force worried that April would become angry with him for staying too long. Scout and Briella left their sanctity beneath the house, and fluttered on the breeze. "Oh look, Force, two butterflies," April said opening the door, giving them access. "Should we try to get them out?"

"No, our skin might affect their wings and stop their ability to fly. Just put the windows down. They will fly out when they are ready," Force replied, getting into the vehicle.

They waved goodbye as April pulled out of the driveway and headed up the road. They travelled to their *special medical centre*, a building that had been constructed to provide specialised care to humans who had been terrorised by creatures and staffed with people with specialised gifts.

April and Force talked about the benefits of having a place in the country. She told him about her concerns, regaling him with stories of her inability to take time out from work. Force encouraged her to think seriously about the proposal. The area was perfect for Scout and he felt that April would learn how to turn off her compunction to capture creatures and allow nature to relax and revitalise her.

They arrived at the centre before any decisions had been made. Force had given her a lot to think about and she would have more than enough time to consider a home in the country while Force examined the processes that had been put in place to assist the children who had been kidnapped. Geoffrey had been the first to be taken by the Jealousy Monsters and therefore, would require the most care.

Force sat on the chair placed near Geoffrey's bed and allowed him to talk about his experience. The boy spoke about the events that led to his feelings of jealousy and he expressed his sorrow that his emotions brought such awful creatures to life.

"How am I supposed to live with the knowledge that I created these monsters?" Geoffrey asked Force. "Look at the emotional damage they have inflicted on the children they tricked into running away from home."

"That was not your fault, Geoffrey. I have had many feelings of jealousy in my lifetime. These monsters could quite easily have been created by me, or anybody else living on the planet," Force replied.

"Yes, but they weren't created by you, were they?"

"No, they weren't. I don't know why things happen to some people and not to others. I do believe, however, in fate, destiny, or whatever else it might be called. There is a reason you and the other children have had to go through this ordeal. We just don't know what it is, yet."

"What good could come of this?" Geoffrey asked him.

"Jacinta's parents have asked the authorities if they could become your foster parents. They are a really lovely couple and they will do everything they can to help you feel safe and cared for."

"Did they really ask to be my parents?"

"Yes, Geoffrey, they did. That has got to make you feel a little better, after everything you have been through, right?"

"I guess. I don't know them."

"No, you don't. But you do know what it is like to not have a place to call home. If you like them, Geoffrey, you will always have a home."

VAMPIRE

Geoffrey sat and mulled over Force's words. He didn't want to feel hope and yet couldn't stop the seed that Force had planted, from beginning to grow. The ringing of Force's phone prevented him from overloading Geoffrey with more things to consider.

"Excuse me, Geoffrey," he said as he stepped outside the room. It was Guardian Karah advising that she had arrived on Earth and was requesting directions to Jacinta's place. Force gave Karah the GPS coordinates to Loretta's place and asked April if she would drive him back to town.

They hadn't been back long when Guardian Karah arrived. She asked to see Jacinta, one of the children who had shown *the signs* that one day she would be a Battle Star on the planet, Mystique. While Karah and Force took care of the girl, April watched the interactions between Loretta, her daughter Calamity, and Jacinta's parents. She concluded Liam would be in good hands if he chose to see where a relationship with this woman would lead.

She hoped Briella was having a good time with Scout, having returned to the area beneath the house. When Karah was finished with Jacinta's memories, she walked out of the room to Jacinta's parents so she could plant some memories in their minds for when their daughter was grown up and whisked away to Mystique. Karah didn't want Jacinta's parents to be devastated when Jacinta left to take her place as a Battle Star, protecting the many universes from the creatures imprisoned there.

"Thank you for pointing out this future Battle Star to me, Liam. I believe she will be a great asset when she comes of age," Karah told him on the front veranda.

"Liam, we forgot about Geoffrey!" April spluttered.

After Liam had strung a few choice words together he said, "Paul and Michelle would like to adopt Geoffrey. He will find it upsetting and confusing if they begin discussing holidays they have spent with Jacinta and not him. What memories did you set in place? I will fix this as soon as I am able to spend some time with them."

Karah melded with his mind and showed him what she had envisaged. She gave them a quick smile, descended the stairs and disappeared when they weren't looking.

April and Liam returned to their friends and said their goodbyes, too. As they made their way to the car, April asked, "Can I give you and Scout a lift somewhere?"

"Nope, they are coming with us," Briella said, fluttering in front of April's face.

"We are going to help them catch a vampire," Scout said, hovering in front of Force's face, with hands on hips and a huge grin on her face.

The Gatherers raced the Locator fairies to the car. April put the car into gear and floored the accelerator. Night had fallen and the vampire was awake, expectant and hungry.

Sixteen

They were an hour from Bastian's place and two hours from the place Sarina was expecting to find Toren. April discovered she was thrilled that Scout had offered Force's help with this mission. She was torn between following the instructions she had been given and doing what she knew to be right. There was a vicious vampire hurting innocent people and she had been told to stand down.

April felt that if she discussed the facts with Force and the Locators, they would be able to help her make the right decision; follow orders or get the vampire. April looked in her rear-view mirror to see what the fairies were currently up to.

Briella and Scout were sitting on the parcel shelf in front of the rear window. They were still busily catching up with each other. April looked back through the windscreen. The road was long and straight. "Do you have your headset on Briella?" April asked.

Briella had been so excited to have Scout there, she had forgotten their usual routine. She grabbed the headset from the cupboard April had built for her and placed it on her head. Briella took a spare set and handed it to Scout to wear.

"Connected and ready," Briella confirmed.

"That's an affirmative for me, too," Scout giggled. "Will she be able to hear our conversation now?"

"Only if you don't turn the switch off," Briella replied, showing her where the button was.

April smiled as she adjusted the volume on the radio until she could hear the fairies perfectly. "I need your help with a dilemma. The vampire we have been tracking is called Sarina and she is the Queen of the Vampires on the planet, Mystique."

"Who told you that?" Force asked.

"It is true, Force, just listen," Briella encouraged.

"She has escaped from Mystique, although nobody can explain how that happened. My first face to face with her occurred on Wednesday night at a park where she had taken the lives of more than twenty people. She told me her name was Sarina, Queen of the Vampires in the Land of Darkness on Mystique. She then proceeded to inform me that she knew Queen Adair had decreed that we not harm the creatures we gathered and suggested I contact my superiors to verify the validity of her statement. She wanted them to locate the Gatherer who captured her during The Cleanse and have him appear at the same park our discussion took place or she would kill over a thousand people." April stopped to get her breath. She didn't realise how much the last few days had affected her.

"I'm guessing from your tone that her statement has been verified," Force asked.

"Yes, it has. I spoke to Toren yesterday. He was just as surprised as I was that she had somehow gotten back to Earth, and he hopped in a chopper to come to help me take care of her. The helicopter crashed, seriously injuring him and killing the pilot."

"April, can you pull over so we can talk about this?"

"No, I am fine."

"No, you are swerving all over the road."

April pulled over and put her hazard lights on.

"Oh my God, Force, they took Toren back to Mystique to recover and that vampire killed hundreds of people at the Convention and Exhibition Centre last night because he didn't show and I followed orders."

"What do you mean, followed orders?" Force asked sharply.

"I have been ordered to protect the family across the street from the house she took as her base and am to leave the gathering of the vampire to Toren when he returns."

"Who gave those orders?"

"Apparently, the Queen."

"Adair or Sarina?"

"Queen Adair."

"Screw that," Force replied. "We are going to take down that vamp, Toren or not. We swore an oath to keep the inhabitants of this planet safe, and that is what we are going to do!"

"I'll agree to that," Scout said. "Take that predator down."

"Briella, what do you think?"

"You already know what I think. I watched you looking out the window last night waiting for Sarina to return. You looked heartbroken. I don't think you could survive another night of Sarina's mayhem. There's been no word on Toren. Like Force said, you swore an oath to the people on Earth to keep them safe. Let the Queen rant and rave after you have caught Sarina and sent her sorry-self home."

April turned her attention back to driving. She checked her mirrors before pulling back onto the road. She would have enjoyed being able to see the change in scenery. She was used to living in the city and it would have been nice to see the wide open spaces dotted with trees and animals instead of tall concrete structures. The drive under the veil of darkness was boring and her mind began to drift.

Everything was so dark out there. April realised how many stars were hidden from view in the city by light pollution. The sky looked amazing and she wished she was able to see this view every night before going to bed. She thought again about the property that was up for sale in the town they had just left. She had quickly discussed with Force the possibility of them sharing a holiday house in the country. She hoped they would be able to view the property soon and find it suitable for their needs. Regardless of whether this property was right for her, she had decided she would be purchasing a home far away from the city, in the near future.

There weren't any street lights on the roads they were traversing to get to the highway. If she had to travel them every evening from her job to her home, it probably would have been enough to put her off the idea of buying in the outskirts. As it was to be a place of relaxation and rest, the need to travel on darkened roads at night was not an issue. April suddenly realised she had not discussed the idea with Briella.

"Briella, there's something else I want to ask your opinion on."

"What is it?" she asked.

"What do you think about the idea Force and I were discussing in the car going to the medical centre?"

"What are you talking about? Scout and I were so busy catching up, we weren't listening to you."

"How would you feel about buying a holiday house in that town we just left?"

"Are you serious? There is nothing to do there!"

"That is the whole point. It is a safe place where you could take some time out to revitalise your spirit and prepare yourself for the next job. Scout would be based there and you two could catch up when you are not working."

"Hey Scout, you didn't tell me you were moving out there!" Briella pouted.

"I didn't know. Force didn't say anything to me about moving," she replied thinking about the kiss that had occurred between Force and Loretta earlier that day.

"It's not definite. Just something April and I were tossing around earlier," Force replied surprised by Scout's angst. "We won't take a look, Scout, if you don't want to. You are quite welcome to stay where you are. I just thought you might have liked it better there with the forest and creek so close to the property for sale. Well, that and the fact that the town is right smack in the middle of the surrounding districts giving you the perfect opportunity to make your stake. I know how much you hate the coastal suburbs."

"How often would you come and stay, April?" Scout asked.

"As often as we could," April replied, "I would need to bring another house for Briella to stay in while she was there. Would you have any objections?"

"Hell, no!" Scout said with excitement.

Force moved his head to the side and looked at April. He saw her sitting beside him with the biggest grin on her face. For the first time since catching up with her, she looked happy.

VAMPIRE

A woman suddenly appeared in the beams of the headlights. April slammed on the brakes and fought the instinct to swerve. Her car wasn't going to stop in time. Bracing for the bang, she was relieved to discover the woman had jumped out of the way just before the bumper bar hit her.

As April and Force were flung forward, they were suddenly stopped by their seatbelts, preventing serious injuries. Unfortunately, the Locator Fairies were not so lucky. They didn't have any safety features in place in the event of an incident. The leather beneath them suddenly disappeared as inertia propelled them through the vehicle.

The rear seats became a blur before they passed April and Force in the front of the car, then became plugged in the air vents. Briella had entered bottom first, finding herself doubled over and in danger of placing her feet in her mouth. Scout's body had been flipped as she passed through an updraft of air from the rolled down window. She ended up in the vent face first, becoming wedged by her hips.

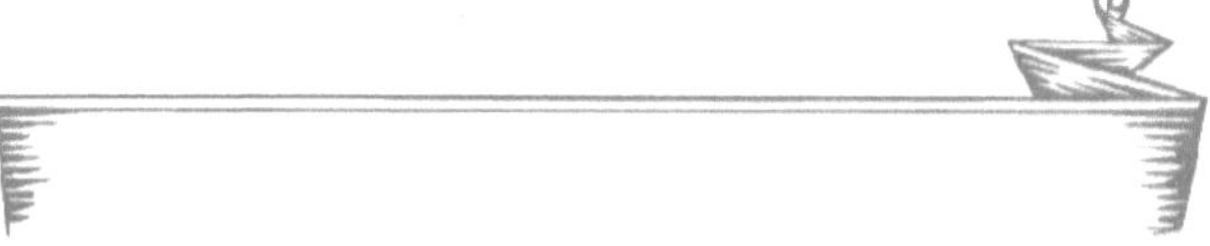

Seventeen

Scout and Briella screamed more out of embarrassment and indignation than pain. They were annoyed to find they had become entangled in such a predicament. No amount of wiggling would free them from their new bonds. The girls grunted and groaned in frustration at being immobilised.

April took a few minutes to orient herself before realising the Locators were currently wedged in her air vents. Briella was yelling obscenities while grabbing hold of her feet to keep them still. Scout's little legs were going up and down like the blades on a pair of scissors slicing through a piece of paper. April couldn't hear Scout's voice through the radio, but she was pretty sure there were some choice words coming out of her mouth as well. The Gatherers used their mind-link capabilities to communicate with the girls.

"*Oh my goodness,*" April said, startled by the picture in front of her, "*are you girls all right?*"

"*What do you think?*" Briella grumbled. "*Get us out of here!*"

"*Will I hurt you?*" April asked with a concerned tone.

"*You can hardly leave us in here, April, so does it really matter?*" mumbled Scout testily.

"Wait!" Force commanded. "You might hurt them if you pull them out. Turn the fan on as high as it will go. Make sure you turn the air conditioner off first. You don't want to burn their delicate skin."

"What will that accomplish?" April asked.

"Hopefully, it will blast them out safely. Ready. Go," he said holding his hand up like a catcher's mitt.

Two little fairies shot out of the vents and into his hand. "Ow, my wrist," Briella complained.

"Well, maybe you should have kept your hands down and let your face make contact with my skin instead," he replied with sarcasm at her ungrateful attitude.

"Thanks, Force," Scout said appreciatively.

"Are you okay, Scout? Are your wings good?" he asked holding his hand out flat and looking at her carefully.

"Yes, I am fine," she replied, "but my side hurts a little."

Scout pulled up her shirt to reveal the beginnings of a very nasty bruise. Force placed his finger a couple of millimetres from her skin and sent out his healing powers. The injury disappeared before their eyes.

"Do you have anything that requires healing, Briella?" he asked.

"No, I am fine, thank you."

"What happened?" Briella asked April.

"I saw a woman in the middle of the road. I thought we were going to hit her," April said with tears in her eyes. Now that the danger had passed, the realisation of what could have been, finally hit her and brought her emotions to the surface. Force suggested she pull off the road and onto the shoulder, so they could get some fresh air and stretch their legs for a few minutes. April took her foot off the brake and nudged the car onto the shoulder as another car, which had been behind them in the distance, caught up to their position.

"You okay, Love?" the driver called to her.

"Yes thank you," she responded.

"What about your friend?" he questioned, noticing Force sitting beside her.

"He's fine, too," she replied.

"Can I give you a lift somewhere?"

"No thanks, we're good."

With a wave and toot of the horn, the driver continued on his journey.

"How about we stretch our legs for a few minutes and let the adrenaline settle before continuing to our destination?" Force suggested.

"The vampire is awake. We need to get there now!" she said anxiously.

"A few minutes won't make any difference to her next victim. A few minutes to get our adrenalin under control will go a long way to us arriving safely to help the unprotected humans," he said.

April thought his words made sense although she was loathe to take time out for something she considered unnecessary. She thought it would be easier to appease him by complying, than have him asking her every few minutes if she was okay. To prevent an accident, April turned the hazards lights on, turned the headlights off but left the parkers on, before exiting the vehicle. She walked around to the passenger side and took Force's outstretched hand in her own. They walked down the embankment in silence, comforted by each other's touch.

Briella and Scout had opted to stay in the car while their Gatherers went for a walk. They watched April and Force through the window as they huddled closely together.

"Wouldn't it be amazing if they fell in love with each other?" Briella said enthusiastically.

"Are you kidding? That would be terrible!" Scout stated.

Briella looked crestfallen. "Don't you like her?"

"I love April," Scout replied with conviction. "That is why I think them falling in love would be a tragedy."

"Why? How could you say such a thing?"

"They would hardly ever see each other. They shouldn't even be working together now. Imagine if they fell in love but couldn't be together. I can't think of anything crueller than that."

Briella thought about what Scout had said and ended up agreeing, although she couldn't shake the feeling that their union would be a wonderful thing. Surely more Gatherers than Rochelle and Toren fell in love from time to time. Yes, they were genetically modified humans that were immortal and sterile, but surely that didn't mean that they couldn't fall in love and have a relationship. It seemed to work okay for Toren and Rochelle. Why not April and Force?

Locator Fairies did not have relationships. On the odd occasion they felt the need to procreate, they would find a partner and have a baby fairy which would then be taken back home to Fairyland to be raised by the fairy community.

It was forbidden by the Queen of Mystique for two Gatherers to become involved in a loving relationship with each other. There were no rules about liaisons between Gatherer and human. Briella still hoped that something would happen between April and Force. She could feel the positive energy that flowed between the pair whenever they were in close proximity to each other and thought it was a waste to let something so special fall by the wayside.

April and Force made their way back to the car. Both of her arms were linked with one of his as they chatted happily with one another. Scout had never really noticed the connection that existed between April and Force, but then she had not noticed the feelings she had for him herself until that morning. Scout wasn't sure how she felt about the whole thing.

They were halfway to the car when Sarina revealed herself. She stood between them and the safety of the silver in the boot of the car. April and Force flicked their hands. A fireball appeared in each palm. The Gatherers were ready for a fight.

"I thought you might have been Toranthian but I can see I was wrong," Sarina said to Force.

"What do you want with him?" Force asked.

"I want to make him mine. Your Battle Stars on Mystique killed my mate Karayan. Toranthian is going to take his place with your Queen's blessing. I want him. Where is he?"

"He is on Mystique," April told her.

"He was supposed to have been returned by now," Sarina told her as she checked April's mind for confirmation. Sarina growled in anger as she learned Adair had not yet allowed him to return. She ran for the portal that would return her to Mystique. She made good time, arriving in two and a half hours. She called to Adair and waited impatiently for a response. As Sarina didn't expect to stay on Earth, she kept her mind open. There was no point in keeping her location secret from the Gatherers. The grass beneath her feet died as she paced backwards and forwards. When she had nearly reached the end of her tether, the portal opened and Queen Adair stepped through with Toranthian.

"You sure took your sweet time!" Sarina snarled.

"We are here, Sarina, isn't that what you wanted?" Adair countered coolly.

"Are you going to give me any trouble?" Sarina asked Toranthian.

"No. I have been apprised of your situation and come willingly to your way of life," he replied.

"You are not even going to put up a little bit of a struggle to keep your life the way it is?" Sarina queried disbelievingly.

"Will I still see you as you appear to me now or will I see the real you beneath the illusion?"

"You will see me however you wish to see me, my love."

"I am ready then. Do what you must."

"We will need to travel to the home I have been using whilst on Earth. I have selected a very special blend to initiate you into the life of a vampire. There is not enough time to bring him to you," Sarina stated.

"That will not be possible. You can begin the process here then step through the portal, where as many humans as you require will be provided. Or you will step through the portal and begin the process on Mystique. Your choice, but make it quick."

"What is the hurry? The sun won't be up for a few hours yet," Sarina questioned.

"Toranthian is not staying on Earth once you have infected him with your blood. I am not taking the risk of any of our other Gatherers becoming infected, nor the humans having confirmation of your existence," Adair responded.

"You will come with me to the house I have been staying in and you will accept the gift I have saved for you. The blood type is extremely rare and it will be a long time before you will get a chance to experience the delicacy again.

"How old is my gift, Sarina? Toren asked.

"Old enough to give you the sustenance you need to begin the change."

"That is not what I asked. How old?"

"Seventeen."

"Not even an adult. I will not begin my new life being a monster, even though I am to become one. Queen Adair, please ensure my first meal is someone who has at least made it to forty years of age. Preferably, someone who has an incurable disease."

"What a bleeding heart you are, my love. Vampirism will soon cure you of that." Sarina took a step forward and stopped when she picked up the sound of a roaring engine. "It seems we have company."

Eighteen

"**H**urry up and bite him!" Adair squealed. "They cannot know I have sanctioned this."

Sarina was afraid she would miss her opportunity and didn't need further bidding. She embraced him as her fangs sank deeply into his jugular vein. She had almost drained him when April and Force came to a stop.

"No," April screamed as she exited the vehicle. Force was already out of the car and running. Adair placed herself protectively between Force and Sarina.

"Force, stop!" she commanded. He went to sidestep her to get to his target. She raised her hands and pushed the air between herself and Force. He flew backwards, landing on his bottom. Force leaned backwards and flipped himself to his feet. He had a new adversary, the Queen herself.

"April," the Queen said calmly.

"*Force, you have to stop,*" April said through mind-link. His feet faltered and he nearly stumbled. "*Please, Force.*"

He looked at her and saw the tears streaming down her face. Force looked at the Queen and saw the determination written all over hers. "I don't understand," he told Adair.

"I know you don't, Force. Sarina was here when we arrived. I should have been more vigilant but didn't think to check for danger. She was on him before I knew it."

"She is going to kill him and you are just standing there, allowing it to happen," he said disillusioned.

"I know how it looks Force, but you cannot kill her and I know you want to. Every vampire on Mystique belongs to Sarina. She is their maker and they have to follow her instructions. If you kill her, there will be no controlling the vampires on Mystique. Every Battle Star will be in danger of becoming a vampire and will find themselves beholden to the one who changes them. As soon as she bit Toren, it was too late for him. You can either find a human that will sustain him through the change or let him go. As for Sarina, I have to take her back to Mystique with me."

"Oh my God, what a nightmare," April expelled.

"Let me see if I've got this straight," Force said looking at Adair. "You want us to choose to save our friend from becoming a vampire by letting him die or kill an innocent human so he can continue to exist, but as a vampire?"

"Clock is ticking," Sarina interjected. "If Toranthian does not feed on a human within the next half an hour, he will not survive the transformation." She didn't bother looking at them. She knew the impact her words would have. Sarina's eyes never left Toren. She used one of her claws to open a vein on her arm and placed it to Toren's lips. He drank hungrily.

Force got out his phone. As soon as Samuel answered, he said, "Ping my phone and find me a criminal living within a ten-kilometre radius."

"There are no criminals on record," Samuel stated.

"Dammit! How could you let this happen?" he roared at Adair. Force grabbed April's arm and they began running. He had picked up a woman a few minutes away and didn't want to run the risk of not finding another in the time limit they had been given. He tried to remove his emotions from his actions. There would be plenty of time to regret his lack of choices later.

Force would have loved to have taken April somewhere else. It was cruel to make her stay and watch their friend of more than three thousand years become that which they hunted. There just wasn't enough time. Besides, he knew she wouldn't allow him to go through something like this on his own. They reached the woman and she gasped in surprise.

"Sorry, didn't mean to scare you," April said. "We were out on a run and didn't see you."

"That's all right," the woman said, hand to chest. "I didn't see you either. I heard you coming and thought you were an animal."

"Do you have any children?" Force asked.

"That is none of your business," the woman replied.

"He didn't mean anything by it. Having children sometimes makes us a bit more alert to the dangers around us," April stated.

"Really?" the woman asked.

Force and April looked at each other and grabbed an arm each.

The ecstasy rushing through Sarina as Toren suckled from her wrist was heavenly. She closed her eyes and let the feeling wash over her. Her mind catalogued the memories that had been transferred to her through Toren's blood. Her eyes flew open when she came across a young girl who was very similar in appearance to Gemma. This girl was a couple of years younger with paler skin and dark patches beneath her eyes.

She wore a floor length dress with long sleeves and a high collar. The dress was white with a few strands of rope in a range of browns intertwined around the waist, neckline, wrist and hem. Her hair was swept up in a French roll as though she was about to be placed on display yet her feet were bare.

"Who is the girl?" Sarina hissed.

"What girl?" Toren groaned, rolling over clutching his chest as his heart skipped a beat.

"The one with brown eyes, brunette hair and long white dress, from many years ago"

"Persephone," he whispered, with a tortured smile of remembrance.

"Who was she to you?"

"My sister. She was my sister who died of a disease that no longer exists," he panted with pain as his heart began to beat irregularly.

"She has come again, Toren. I have seen her. She is the sister of the one I had kept as a gift for you. Toren, she can live forever now. I will go and get her."

"No! Let her be."

"But, surely it is the wish of Destiny that I should run into her so that you and she could be reunited and live an eternal life together."

"Sarina, how old is she?"

"I don't know. A bit younger than her brother."

"So she is not an adult. If she is to be reunited with me, then it needs to be when she has finished growing."

Sarina considered his words but couldn't see the need to wait. She was about to voice her opinion when she considered something else. Her longing to break her family free of the confines of the prison had escalated to a new level since her arrival on Earth. If he wanted to have the chance to be with his reincarnated sister then he would be more likely to help her develop an effective strategy of escape.

If the vampirism affected him as she hoped it would, he may even help her begin a revolution to unite all the creatures imprisoned on the planet. Sarina felt her heart quicken with excitement and heard Toren's groans of pain as the potency of her adrenalin hit his stomach. He threw his head back and screamed in agony.

Sarina wanted to tell him what it was like on Mystique and how she wanted to change things. She kept her head and thoughts to herself. There was no way she was going to discuss those sort of things in front of the Queen to the Battle Stars. Now she just wished the Gatherers would hurry and bring the sacrifice to Toren to help him with the transformation.

She stroked Toren's forehead with gentle fingers while revelling in his pain. The more painful the transformation, the stronger the vampire he would become. When he had completed his rebirth, she would take a cupful of his blood and mix it with her own. A few drops of the mixture would then be fed to each of her children, ensuring their cooperation and loyalty to their new King. 'What are you thinking, my Toranthian,' she wondered.

Toren could not believe the pain that ravaged his body. It felt as though acid was racing through his veins and arteries, melting everything it touched. His body was burning, his muscles fluctuated between relaxation and contraction, and his head and heart felt as though they were going to explode. His lungs felt like they were working properly, but the oxygen was unable to pass through to the blood. He knew he was going to die, but he fought to hold on anyway.

Nothing he tried calmed his thoughts. None of the mindfulness techniques he had learned over the years helped him deal with the pain. He could hear himself screaming, but couldn't make himself stop. The questions Sarina asked about his sister, Persephone, brought back a flood of beautiful memories of a life which had ended in tremendous feelings of pain, compounding the trauma he already suffered. There was nothing he could cling to, and then, there was the image of Rochelle.

His beloved, with mischievous grey eyes, high cheekbones, plump lips, delicate ears, wide forehead and pointed chin. She had a petite waist, long legs and a chest that made a lovely pillow. Her voice was like the strings on a harp playing in harmony. Her care factor was set to maximum and her love of nature was unquantifiable. She loved going out for Chinese food, eating chocolate chip ice-cream and drinking coffee as though her life depended on it.

They spent as much time together as their jobs allowed. Spending time doing humans things, like going to the movies, sporting events and barbecues in the park. They also enjoyed transforming into animals and soaring through the air, or running through the woods or swimming in the ocean.

As tears rolled down his face, he thought of how much he loved her. He didn't dwell on how much he would miss her. He concentrated on all the wonderful times they had spent together as a couple over the past five centuries. He was roused from his memories by Sarina. "They're here."

April and Force appeared with the screaming woman, struggling between them. They threw the woman towards Toren and apologised for what was about to happen. Sarina approached the woman who shrieked in fear. Her screams were cut short by the pressure of Toren's mouth on her windpipe as his teeth found her jugular. Once he had drained her blood, Adair and Toren stepped through the portal to Mystique.

Sarina smirked at April and Force. "I always get my man," she announced. Raising her hand as April prepared to lunge, Sarina said, "I suppose you know I connected with your mind. I used your mind-linking abilities to boost my own so that I could locate Carl and inform him that his house is of no further use to me. He will wait another two days before making the journey home. My *special* gift to you." Sarina laughed with glee as she stepped through the portal. April and Force tried to follow but found they were blocked from entering.

The couple fell to their knees and howled with grief. Scout and Briella flew to their Gatherers and tried to comfort them as best they could. The four of them sat in the clearing and cried until the sun peeked its head above the horizon. April realised she had not contacted Karen or Walter to let them know she was safe. They would be beside themselves with worry. She contacted Samuel and asked him to connect her to the house.

Bastian answered the phone and told her he had covered for her. He had made up some story about her calling and saying that her car had broken down and the insurance company had put her up in a hotel for the night. April was impressed that he had lied to his parents successfully. She figured he was a pretty straightforward kind of guy, which was probably why his parents had so willingly believed him.

"Have you caught the vampire?" he whispered down the line.

"Sarina has been dealt with."

"What about Mr. Cameron? Is he coming home or is he dead?"

"He should be home in the next couple of days."

"Are you okay, April? You sound as though you've been crying."

"I'm fine. I'll see you later."

April ended the call. "How are we going to tell Rochelle?" she asked, bursting into tears again.

"We'll tell her together. Let's go tie things up with the family you were protecting, then we'll head on over to Rochelle's. It's not something we can tell her over the phone," he said wrapping his arms around her. Force let her cry for a few minutes before guiding her to the car. He helped her into the passenger seat before sliding himself behind the wheel.

Scout and Briella settled themselves onto the parcel shelf but decided to leave the headphones where they were. The fairies didn't feel like talking to the Gatherers and they were pretty sure the Gatherers didn't feel like talking to them, either. Force started the car and headed in the direction indicated by the navigation system.

Nineteen

Force brought the car to a stop as Gemma and Katherine, who had been waiting by the window, hurried to greet them. April looked at Force and felt a small smile tug at the corners of her mouth. She noticed the stress lines around his eyes and reminded him to change the colour of his irises to a dark brown instead of his natural coral colour. The girls opened April's door and helped her to exit the vehicle.

"How did it go?" Gemma asked. "By the look of your red-rimmed eyes, not so good,"

"There were some casualties. The main thing is, Sarina is gone and your family and the rest of humanity are safe, once more," April advised.

"I am so sorry to hear that," Katherine stated. "I mean, I am glad we are safe, but I never once considered that the monsters that you deal with on a daily basis could affect your lives in the same way as those of the victims you protect. Is there anything we can do to help?"

April gave her a hug. "You have helped already."

"Come inside," Gemma encouraged. "We will get you something to eat and drink. Bring Briella, she can stay hidden in my room."

April opened the back door and held out her bag for Briella and Scout. She and Force had some things to take care of and she had no idea how long they would take. She had no intentions of letting the girls know about Scout, but it was too hot, even at this time of the morning, to allow the fairies to wait in the car and with Max in the backyard, that was out of the question as well.

April straightened and closed the door. She turned around and sniffed as she caught a look of sadness on Force's face before he composed himself. He offered her his hand, which she accepted, and they followed the girls into the house. Bastian had just finished making scrambled eggs with tomato, onion, bacon, cheese and toast. He placed glasses of juice on the table, along with the cutlery. He gave a strained smile as his eyes met April's, then stepped forward to shake Force's hand. The group sat at the table and began to eat their food.

April pushed her food around on the plate while Force pushed his sadness aside and enjoyed the food he was consuming. "Rochelle would want you to keep up your strength by eating," he told her.

Bastian and the girls were dying to ask what had happened but were sensitive enough, not to. They wondered who Rochelle was, but came to the conclusion they would probably never know. April placed some food in her mouth, chewed and swallowed. "This tastes great, Bastian."

"Thanks, April."

"Where are your parents?" Force asked.

"At the markets," Bastian replied.

"They'll probably come back with all sorts of useless junk," Gemma stated.

"My parents are always telling me. 'One man's junk is another man's treasure'."

"That's an old saying, Katherine" April replied. "I can't remember who said it, but it has been around for a very long time." Force smiled. April knew who had said it but for reasons known only to her, was keeping the information to herself.

"What are your plans for today, now that Sarina is gone?" Katherine asked quietly.

"As you are aware, we need to modify your memories so that Briella's existence can remain a secret. Katherine, I am afraid you will not be able to remember any of us, at all."

"But I already know about you guys, through Callum."

"That is not exactly true." Force interjected. "You know Callum, and will always remember him, but you would not be able to name or picture anyone else from Starlight Investigations before us, that is."

Katherine thought about what he said and found that to be true. Her shocked face told those in attendance that Force was right. "How are you going to remove yourself from my memories? If Gemma's parents mention you and I don't know who they are talking about, that is going to seem a bit strange, don't you think? Are you going to remove Gemma's memories about Callum? I told her a bit about him and how he helped me when I needed it."

April looked at Force and raised her eyebrows. He was the one that responded. "I guess you can keep those memories, but Briella has to be erased. Not negotiable."

"Thank you," Katherine stated.

"Fine," Gemma responded.

April's phone ringing interrupted the conversation. She didn't recognise the number, "Hello, April speaking."

"Hi, April, it's Michelle Tillie. Have I caught you at a bad time?"

"Hi, Michelle. No, your timing is good. Is everything okay with Jacinta?" she asked, looking directly at Force, whose eyes showed instant concern.

"Jacinta is fine. I am ringing to see if you have had a chance to discuss the property with your husband. It is listed in our local paper for an open house at 11:30 this morning."

"Really? Well then, we had better get a wriggle on if we want to see if it is suitable or not. Liam is working on a new case and won't be able to make it. He and Wade have the same tastes, though, so it shouldn't really make a difference. If we like it, Liam will be happy to go halves. Where shall we meet you?"

"At the property. Give me a ring when you are a few minutes away. Angela, the agent handling the sale, gave me permission to give you an advanced tour if you were interested in having a look and able to get here earlier."

"Wow that was nice of her. It will take us a couple of hours to get there."

"Talk to you soon, then?"

"Yes, we will be there as soon as we can."

April worked quickly and effectively, removing all knowledge of Briella from the trio's minds. She allowed them to remember herself and Force, as discussed and agreed upon previously and then sat down to write a short note to their parents.

Dear Karen and Walter,

The family that I am to live with for the next few weeks have contacted me and asked if I could come now. I wanted to wait for you to arrive home so that I could thank you in person, but they have invited a whole crowd of people to have morning tea with me. You made me feel very welcome, like a member of your family, and I appreciate that more than you could know. Thank you for making my first couple of days in Australia so warm and joyful. I hope that you can find it in your hearts to barrack for me during the Olympics, even if you feel the need to put your Australian swimmers first, LOL.

Thank you once again for your hospitality.

April.

"Can you give this to your parents when they come home?" she asked, handing the note to Bastian.

"Of course. I suppose you are heading off then?" Bastian asked.

"Yes, our job here is done and we are needed somewhere else," April replied.

"Is there another creature?" Gemma asked, wide eyed.

"No, nothing like that. We are catching up with some friends," Force responded.

"Whew, that put a skip in my heartbeat," Katherine stated. Tears sprang into April's eyes before she could stop them. "Did I say something wrong?"

"No, I am just going to miss you all. I had such a good time at the pool. Thank you for providing some great fun."

"You can come back anytime, April," Gemma said, wrapping her arms around April's waist and squeezing her tightly. Katherine joined in, as did Bastian.

"Thank you for protecting my family, April. I don't think it would have turned out so well if you hadn't come," Gemma said.

"You should be thanking Katherine for calling Starlight Investigations and letting them know you were in trouble."

"Don't worry, I have something very special planned to thank Katherine for bringing you into our lives and for sharing a painful part of hers."

April smiled at the girls, then glanced at Bastian. "Well, I need to be off. Take care of each other."

Force took April by the hand and led her to the door. "Bye, kids."

"Bye," they chorused.

Toren's grip was like a vice on Sarina's hand, but that was okay, she could take it. She soothed his forehead with her fingers, tracing the lines as his skin furrowed in response to the pain that wracked his body. "Hush, my darling, it will all be over soon enough," she crooned.

His head turned towards her voice and his eyes latched onto hers. She nodded in approval. His transformation was happening much more quickly than anticipated. Already, his eyes had brightened to a deep burgundy instead of the cloudy dark grey that most would be displaying at this stage. Her new love was to become a very formidable adversary to those who wished to defy their wishes.

"Sarina?"

"Yes, Toranthian. It is I."

"Where are we?"

"At home, on Mystique. You are in our castle." His back arched as a spasm gripped his core muscles. He closed his mouth tightly and refused to give voice to his suffering. "You are so strong, my love," she marvelled.

Toren kept his thoughts to himself. She leaned in closer and listened to his chest. His heartbeat had slowed to a point that it would barely register on an Electrocardiograph. Even from that short distance, she found it difficult to hear the sound that indicated life. His skin had paled significantly and his temperature had cooled considerably. Soon, his old life would cease to exist and his birth into his new life will have been completed. Sarina hissed as she heard the handle of the door being drawn down.

"It is only me, my Queen."

Sarina eyed Gualtiero with some apprehension. While she was the Queen and her children were forced to do her bidding, Gualtiero had always considered himself to be ruler of her army and had wanted to take Karayan's place if the opportunity ever arose. She appreciated his loyalty but could not bring herself to see him as her partner. She knew he waited for the opportunity to challenge Toranthian. He knew that regardless of the outcome of that contest, she would not gift him with being the Father to her children.

"What do you want, Gualtiero?"

"I come bearing gifts for the new King." He reached for something out of sight then pushed a woman into the room. "New blood, courtesy of the Battle Stars. Fresh and clean as requested. They must have liked that one," he said, nodding his head towards Toren.

"Yes, he was one of Adair's favourites, I believe."

"So was choosing him as a replacement for Karayan, a way of alienating her?"

"My reasons for choosing him are my own. They have nothing to do with Adair."

"Really? Come on, Sarina, tell me why you have passed over your most trusted and masterful vampire for that, one of the things that imprisons us on this planet. Have I not given you everything you have asked for and more?"

Toranthian leapt off the bed and launched himself at the woman. He had her in his arms and was feeding from her before Gualtiero had realised he had moved.

"Crap, he's fast. When did you turn him?"

"Not even twelve hours ago. Don't tell me you have forgotten him, Gualtiero. Take a closer look."

Gualtiero took a few side steps to put Toren's face in view. It was a bit hard to tell what he looked like with his eyes closed and his mouth wrapped around the woman's neck. He waited a few seconds for Toren's thirst to be quenched before jumping back in astonishment as Toren looked at him for the first time. "He's the one that captured the two of you, and those of us in the executive team."

"Yes, he is. He also has insider knowledge of how the portals between here and the Earth work, and unlike the losers here, he was able to control each of the elements. It will be interesting to see, once his transformation is complete, whether that is still the case."

"And if it is, will those abilities be passed on to us once we have consumed his blood?"

"We shall have to wait and see."

Toren listened and waited to see if Gualtiero would attempt anything while he was still in a weakened condition. He didn't realise that he was the strongest vampire ever created in history, but Gualtiero was beginning to. Toren had only learned that his transformation was happening faster than anticipated and that the speed with which he moved, startled Gualtiero.

The last piece of conversation had brought his understanding for why Sarina had chosen him in the first place to the fore. She could have chosen any of the Battle Stars on Mystique, but other than the Royals, each of them were only able to control one of the elements. Toren was able to control them all. The fact that he was the one to capture them in the first place was just the icing on the cake.

They hoped that after all was said and done, they would push the evolution envelope and become something even more powerful than they were now. Toren was too far gone to realise the ramifications for the Battle Stars or the humans. He had lost his sense of humanity and only felt a thirst for blood.

"I'm still hungry. Do you have any more?" he asked Gualtiero.

"Sure, follow me."

Toren followed Gualtiero through the upper story of the castle. It was expansive and unnaturally bright. When Adair had come to him and told him what she needed him to do, he had pictured living in a world of gloom. He would never have imagined this. When the castle had been designed and furnished, it had been done so with humans in mind.

Paintings of the vampires adorned the walls, chaises lined the walls for those who wished to lounge, and marbled statues decorated the hallways and staircases. None of these things brought forth sentiments of caring, love or belonging. They were merely objects that required deviation from one's path and cluttered the sleek lines of the castle.

The pair glided down the stairs and out the front doors. The night was cool and the full moon cast a bright glow across the land. There were no houses to ruin the landscape. Open spaces, wooded areas and a system of caves made up their countryside.

Situated on the western side, the portal, offered the only entrance and exit to the Land of Darkness as the borders were protected by an integrated structure of powerful crystals. A gentle breeze caressed their faces bringing a smorgasbord of scents to their notice. Toren searched the area for his prey. His newly enhanced eyes spotted a woman with a long, blonde braid in the distance reminding him of Rochelle. His instincts kicked in and the hunt began. All thoughts of testing his abilities fled as his hunger took over.

Sarina was euphoric. He was a natural vampire, the best she had ever seen. "My children, come meet your new father," she said, as Toren returned to her side. Vampires swarmed from every corner of the country. They gathered before her and waited patiently for her to speak. "Children, meet my new mate, Toranthian. Drink of our blood and become stronger than you have ever been before."

Sarina dragged her claw through her wrist and held it over the chalice. After a few minutes, she sealed it closed with her saliva, then Toren repeated the process. Unbeknownst to her, the blood that ran into the chalice from him was blood that had been collected and placed into a vial soon after he had arrived on Mystique for treatment, after being injured in the helicopter incident.

Once Toren and Queen Adair had arrived in the Land of Darkness after he had been bitten, she slipped him the vial and told him to punch a hole in his skin with the needle she had given him, and place it inside the vial. The virus being passed by blood passing through the needle, would change the blood in the vial.

It had been tampered with by the Restorers, in the hopes of reshaping his DNA strands, back to what they were before he became a Battle Star. The Restorers hoped that, once the vampires drank the mixture of combined blood, they would still be beholden to him, but would not have access to his special abilities, or to the fairy dust that had become a part of him.

Toren watched Sarina offer up the chalice to each of her children. A small whirlwind whizzed over the landscape, bringing a smile to his lips and a sparkle to his eyes.

Twenty

It was a completely different experience travelling the country roads in the daylight. Previously, the most the Gatherers could see were the multitude of stars in the sky. This time, they were able to see the farm animals scattered throughout the paddocks, the tall wispy grasses and the barbed wire fences that ran through them. There were more opportunities for spotting kangaroos and other wildlife venturing across the road, giving them a greater chance of survival. April engaged cruise control to ensure the car sat on the speed limit.

Force turned his gaze to April. "We are nearly there. Are you sure you want to have a holiday home in the country?"

"No, not really. It is probably too quiet and there isn't much to do, but that is the whole point, isn't it? I need to learn to power down."

"Yes, I have to agree with that. You have been a dynamo ever since the change. Always working or looking for something to do. It is good to relax every once in a while."

"Why? My body renews itself regardless. We haven't aged since we underwent radiation therapy. Sometimes I get tired of living forever and watching everyone else die. When I am left to my thoughts, that is where they always turn to."

"There are a lot of beautiful things that you should take the time to appreciate, April. Nature is a beautiful thing to behold. People are wondrous creatures to interact with. The weather is an awesome entity to study. You just need to become aware of it all to become totally immersed in the miracle of it all."

April glanced at him incredulously. "How long have you been preparing that little speech?"

"Came up with it just now?" he grinned. April couldn't help it, she smiled, too.

"I am sure that Briella and I will grow to love it, wherever we decide to buy." She turned down the road leading to the centre of town. "Wade darling, don't forget your eyes are brown."

"Right, I am Wade, your loving husband," he said as his eyes changed shade. "Can you swing by the Pub so I can check on my bike? We can ring Michelle, from there to let her know we have arrived."

April nodded. "We should see about catching up with Geoffrey so we can implant those memories that Guardian Karah shared with you."

"We will need to modify Michelle's and Paul's as well. The future memories buried deep inside their minds for when Jacinta is sent to Mystique to become a Battle Star will also need to include Geoffrey."

April pulled in beside Force's bike. He climbed out of the car while April pulled her phone out of her bag. She dialled Michelle's number and received directions to the property for sale. Force took a few minutes to check on his stuff then climbed back into the car. He handed April a bottle of soft drink that he had collected from the bar fridge in his room.

"Thanks. Michelle and Paul are going to meet us at the property. She asked if it would be a problem if she brought Geoffrey along. Jacinta is spending the day with Calamity, can you believe that?"

"I don't know whether to be happy or concerned. Up until yesterday, Calamity was so determined to make sure that none of her friends would give Jacinta the time of day, and here she is playing with her, herself. I know I told Calamity that Jacinta helped save her from Ruby and Lucas, but this complete turnaround is a little quick, don't you think?"

"I think we should accept it for what it is; a girl who was consumed with jealousy who no longer feels that way. Let's just wait and see how their relationship pans out. In the meantime, it gives us the perfect opportunity to carry out our duties."

She pulled out of the carpark and within ten minutes, they were pulling into the driveway to the house that soon might be theirs. It was like the other homes in the area: a Queenslander that had a veranda on three sides, the bedrooms at the front and the living areas and kitchen at the back.

The house was built on ten acres which did not currently house any livestock. The acre around the home was cleared of trees and shrubs, which made it safer in a bushfire, and easier to see snakes that might be passing through. Towards the back of the property was a wooded area, similar to the one where Ruby and Lucas had taken the kidnapped children.

April and Force placed their hands on the ground and felt the layout of the parts they couldn't see with their eyes. A stream ran through the middle of the forest and there were a number of burrows and underground systems, most likely belonging to a family of wombats. Force swung his head around and pointed to the car coming their way. "Michelle, Paul and Geoffrey." They walked to the front of the property and waited at the bottom of the stairs.

"Good morning, guys," Force said as they exited the vehicle.

"Good morning, April, Wade," Paul said, extending his arm for a handshake.

Michelle hugged them both and Geoffrey stood back, a little unsure of himself.

"G'day mate, how'd you sleep last night?" Force asked.

"Yeah, good. Here's the keys."

Force took them from Geoffrey and placed his hand on the boys shoulder. "April, my brother, and I are looking for a holiday home. How about you show me around and give me your thoughts on this place."

The boys wandered off to poke their noses into every nook and cranny. April and Michelle decided to let them go, preferring to do their own inspection without the emotional excitement of boy stuff. She knew Force was already considering building a waterfall out the back for Scout and to bring in even more wildlife to the area. He wanted to reshape other areas as well but would put that on hold until he had lived there for a year and seen the flow of the four seasons on their block of dirt.

Michelle kept an eye on April peripherally. She noted the change in posture and movement from the previous night and wondered if she should say something. The only interaction she had managed to have with April was when she had come to let Force know that the kidnapped children had been taken to a medical centre for observation and the local children had been given the all clear to return home to their parents. Paul and Michelle had been allowed to collect Geoffrey that morning and bring him home. First thing in the morning, they would be finalising the paperwork to become Geoffrey's foster parents. Being the woman Michelle was, she had to see if there was something she could do to help.

"Is everything okay, April?"

"Yes, thank you, Michelle," April smiled.

"Both you and Wade were happy to come and view the property?"

"Yes." April frowned slightly and her smile faltered.

"I am sorry for fussing. I like to help people and I have the feeling something is bothering you immensely."

"It is quiet here," April replied as a way of explaining everything.

"Yes, it is part of the charm of the place."

"There would be a lot of time to think here."

"Are you worried to be alone with your thoughts, April?"

"Of course, aren't you?"

"Heavens, no. Sometimes you need quiet to be able to figure out what is important and worth fighting for, and what you can let go of without regret. Are you and Wade okay?"

"Yes, we are fine. We lost a dear friend last night. When we are finished here, we will need to go and see his partner and let her know."

"She doesn't know already?"

"No, she knows he was injured. We haven't had the chance to tell her there was a further complication. She is working a case and mobile coverage is currently unavailable. I am not looking forward to telling her and don't know if I can even hold it together to tell her." The tears flowed freely and April became frustrated with her inability to hold her emotions in check. She wiped the tears from her face with a handkerchief.

"You will tell her as gently as you can and you will have a cry together. There is nothing wrong with grieving, April. It is a heart wrenching thing to say goodbye to a loved one and it needs to be with others who feel the same way. Imagine if she were to find out from some stranger knocking on her door or on the end of a phone line. You are the best person to tell her and I am sorry that you are the one who has to do it," Michelle said, gently rubbing April's arm in support.

"Thank you, Michelle," April sniffed. "God, Wade is going to be so upset when he sees me like this."

"Only because you are hurting, as he will be, too. Lean on each other for support. It will get you through this tough time and will bring you even closer together. Now, how about we take a look at the inside of the house? Wade is going to want to know what you think, and I am sure Liam will ask for and value your opinion, more than his brother's."

As they viewed the property, April wondered how she would feel if she lost Force. They weren't romantically connected and never had been in the past. He had always felt like her brother and she knew she would be devastated if he were to die. Perhaps more so, as they were pretty well indestructible.

She could not imagine the pain Rochelle was going to feel when they told her Toren was gone. They were an intimate part of each other's lives and had been for over five centuries. The girls reached the back of the house and found the boys squashed into the small kitchen.

"A bit small," Force grimaced, when he saw them.

"Hmmm," April replied.

"We could extend the veranda so that it surrounds the entire house, or better still, build a large deck. Then you could either enlarge the existing kitchen or build an outside kitchen on your new deck," Paul suggested.

"Like at Loretta's place," Michelle responded. "It was lovely having our barbecue dinner there. We should look at doing something similar at our place, Paul."

"I'll look into it and see if I can find a reputable builder in the area," he replied.

"What about the builders connected to the estate?"

"I'd prefer to keep our work life and private life separate. We will find a builder who focuses on restoration projects. That way, the deck should look as though it has always been part of the house and not a tacky add-on."

April and Force took in the way Geoffrey watched his new foster parents. He was a troubled fourteen year old who had been passed from one family to another. For the past six months he had been imprisoned by a pair of monsters created out of the incredibly powerful feelings of jealousy that Geoffrey had housed deep within himself. As his feelings had deepened, the creatures had grown in strength until they had managed to capture another five children.

Once Scout had picked them up on her radar, it was a race to save their next target, Calamity, from being captured and to find and release the other children. Geoffrey not only suffered from feelings of inadequacy, he was dealing with feelings of guilt over being responsible for the other children being imprisoned alongside him.

"So, what do you think, Geoffrey? Should we buy the place?" Force questioned. "I have a feeling you might like to have a go at restoring a place yourself."

"I'm pretty handy with a hammer and set of nails. I like to make things when I am feeling unhappy."

"How many things have you made, Geoffrey?" Michelle queried.

"Lots," he responded.

"Well, then, let's see if you are still able to use your skills when you are happy, because we are not planning on having you moping around and feeling as though you don't belong," Paul stated. "Want these two as neighbours, or not?"

"Yeah, I think this place has real potential and is reasonably priced. I would be happy to help you fix her up, if you would be happy to have me around. There is lots I don't know, but I am a quick study."

"You don't have to sell yourself to us, mate. We are pretty good at sizing people up, and you, my friend, are a good egg. I am taking your response to mean that you are recommending we buy the place?" Geoffrey nodded his head. "Then I guess you had better call Angela and ask her if we can place a deposit on the house and sign some forms before somebody else decides to buy it at the open house."

April mind-linked with Briella, perched in her handbag with Scout. 'What do you think?'

'Scout and I are thrilled. We have decided it would be good to live here. Can you make Scout a house? Not like mine, maybe something more tree shaped, or like a mushroom.'

'Force is going to take Scout's house with him to the house. They are going to base themselves here, remember. She won't need a second house, like you. I am going to build you another one, for when we come and stay a couple of days. Unless you would prefer to camp in the woods.'

'You can make me a mushroom shaped house if you like.'

'Okay, Briella. You can help me draw up the plans when we get home.'

Michelle walked downstairs to the car and grabbed a basket from the boot of the car. "We hoped you would decide to buy the place, so we packed some extra food for our picnic celebration."

"What if we had declined to buy?"

"Paul and I were planning on taking Geoffrey down to the river near the park to celebrate his becoming part of our family. But I figure, correct me if I am wrong, Geoffrey's mind will be racing with ideas he can give you on how to make this place more comfortable and he would be happier to stay here."

"Thanks, Michelle. I would prefer to stay here to eat lunch," Geoffrey said surprised that she had read him so well.

While Paul spread out the picnic blanket and Michelle unpacked the basket, Force accessed the memories Karah had implanted and added

Geoffrey into the mix. They both swiped at their faces to chase away non-existent insects upon entry and exit to their minds.

April lowered her eyes with a smile and found an actual ladybug on her thigh. This reminded her the fairies were still inside her handbag and she opened it carefully so as not to bring attention to her actions. The girls flew out quickly, heading away from the group before circling back to take cover beneath the house. From there they flew to the wooded area in search of mushrooms and a drink from the stream.

Michelle placed the chicken and pasta salad rolls on one plate and the ham and coleslaw rolls on another, for people to make their own choice. There were bottles of juice, soft drink and water in a cooler with slices of carrots and celery plus containers of various dips.

While Geoffrey ate, Force planted a number of memories to be released at appropriate times pertaining to non-existent holidays he would take with Jacinta throughout his lifetime. A cruise to the Whitsundays for her eighteenth birthday. A ski trip to the Himalayas for his twenty-first and a trip to Canada for hers. A wedding when she turned twenty-five and they would catch up with them all to implant more memories as they became older. They had just finished eating when Angela arrived to accept their cheque for ten thousand dollars as a deposit and to sign the paperwork.

April and Force asked for a two week contract. They weren't interested in conducting a building or pest inspection. They could tell the property wasn't infested and they could manipulate the materials used to build the house as required with their control over the elements. Angela placed an under contract sticker over the For Sale sign but explained that the open house would still need to proceed in case the sale fell through. April and Force were not the least bit concerned. Angela excused herself to prepare for the open house. The five of them packed up the picnic and placed the leftovers and rubbish in the boot.

Force shook each of their hands. "Thank you for a lovely lunch and the opportunity to become a part of this wonderful community."

"We should be thanking you, April and your brother Liam for making our children safe. It could have been Jacinta who was taken instead of Calamity, you know," Paul said.

"Gosh, I shudder to think what could have happened," Michelle remarked, reaching out for Geoffrey's hand. "You brought us Geoffrey. You saved him from those monsters and gave us the son we could never have. We will be eternally grateful." She gave Force a kiss on his cheek. "Come and see us soon." Then she gave April a kiss, "Good luck, Love, with your friend. I will be thinking of you and am here if you need a shoulder to cry on or someone who will just listen and understand what you are going through. I lost a daughter seven months ago. I am here if you need me."

"Thank you, Michelle." April hugged her tightly, blinking back the tears. They climbed into their car with Geoffrey hanging out the window, waving enthusiastically.

Briella and Scout heard the wheels on the gravel and flew to the Gatherers. Scout perched on Force's shoulder while Briella landed on April's.

"We need to contact Rochelle and set up a meeting," April said.

"Let's go back to my place at the Pub. We can ring from there and make the arrangements."

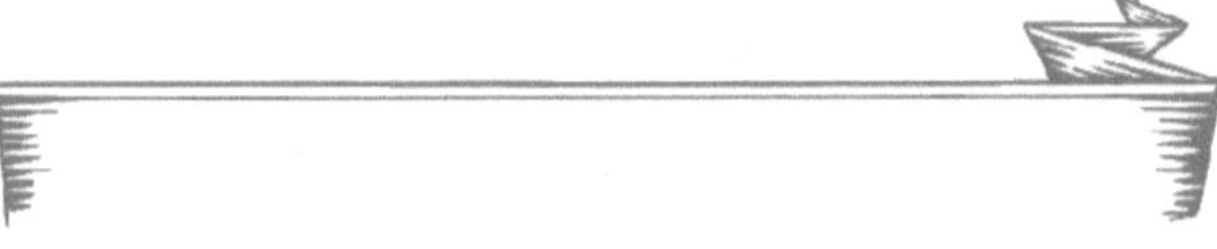

Twenty-One

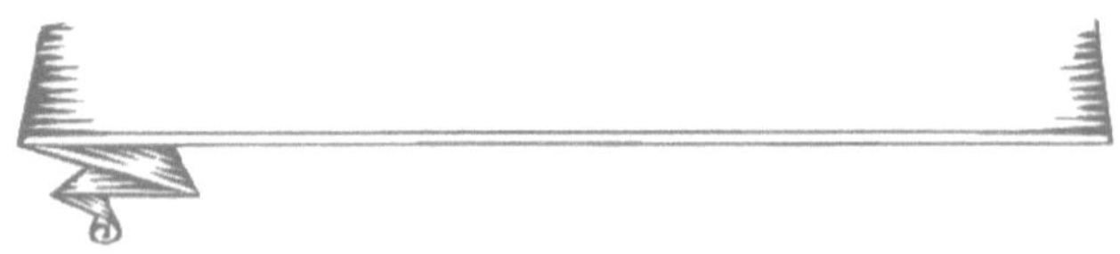

The portal between Earth and the planet, Mystique, opened, bringing forth two visitors. Guardians Elden and Manuel stepped through the doorway and took stock of their surroundings. As their arrival was not expected, they did not concern themselves with the normal conventions of being on Earth. Elden raised his hand with his thumb and index finger touching. He allowed them to separate and by doing so, created a temporary doorway between the clearing that housed the portal and the yard of the house that Rochelle currently worked in.

The Guardians stepped through this new doorway and arrived at their destination within seconds. They could hear Rochelle talking to herself which meant she was feeling frustrated by her current situation. Elden looked for confirmation from Manuel that they were doing the right thing by the Gatherer. She was to be given a most difficult task and they were unsure they would survive her initial reaction to the assignment. Realising they couldn't put their meeting off any longer, they approached the house.

There were no humans present in the dwelling which meant they would not have to worry about innocents becoming caught in the crossfire. Elden felt it would be better to announce their presence before entering the building. Elden and Manuel didn't have the same power over the elements as Rochelle did. Elden was a Dampier and was only able to control the element of water. Manuel was a Restorer and was able to heal the injured. He wished with all his heart he had the ability to heal Rochelle's. That was one thing he wasn't able to do. Only time would be able to take care of that.

"Rochelle, it's Guardians Elden and Manuel. May we come in?" he called to her.

Rochelle poked her head through the window opening. "What are you two doing here?" she asked. When they didn't answer right away, she said, "How about I come out? I have a feeling I am not going to like what you have to say." She made her way downstairs with trepidation. 'It is unusual enough for Elden, the King's Guardian, to make his way to Earth, but to bring another Guardian? Something big is going on,' she thought.

Rochelle opened the door and exited the house. Her mind raced with lots of possibilities that would explain their arrival, but instead of blurting them out and playing the guessing game, she kept herself calm and waited.

She stood eye to eye with them and then wished she hadn't. They were worried, and her natural instincts kicked into gear.

Elden's usual posture of authority was off. He was portraying a man who was unsure of the outcome of this meeting and was ready to flee. His dark brown eyes seemed haunted, and his mouth had a slight downward curve instead of the approachable, closed-mouth smile he usually displayed when dealing with the Gatherers. His shoulders were shifted slightly forward beneath his Guardians uniform which was similar to that of the Queen's, except his was aquamarine, whereas hers was ruby coloured. A small furrow formed between his eyebrows as he contemplated once again, how to begin the conversation with Rochelle.

"Rochelle, there has been an incident involving Toranthian," Elden said quietly.

"Yes, I know. April rang and told me his helicopter went down. Is it going to take a bit longer for him to come home?"

"What do you mean?" Elden queried.

"What are you talking about?" Rochelle countered.

"Toranthian is on Mystique," Elden stated.

"Yes, I know. He was taken there after his helicopter accident to prevent medical people here asking awkward questions about his healing abilities," Rochelle responded.

"It's a little more complicated than that," Manuel said.

"I'm sorry, who are you?" Rochelle asked, looking him over. He had short black hair, dark eyes and a wide chin. He was a lot broader than Elden and appeared to have a beer belly.

"Guardian Manuel, Head Guardian of the Restorers."

"What is a Restorer?"

"A Battle Star that can heal," he answered.

"We can all heal," Rochelle stated.

"Rochelle, the Battle Stars on Mystique are not like the Gatherers on Earth. They cannot control all of the elements like you. When they go through the transfer process, they are given control over one element only," Elden explained.

"Okay, so why are you telling me this now?"

"Do you want to sit down?" Manuel asked, feeling really nervous now they had gotten to the crux of the matter.

"No, I don't want to sit down! One of you had better tell me what is going on before I lose my temper," she said irritably.

"Toranthian will not be returning home anytime soon," Manuel answered.

"Why not? April said he would be returning today at the latest," Rochelle spluttered. "I told her the Queen would not return him, if she managed to get him away from here. She doesn't approve of us having a relationship, preferring us to deal with the loss of a human every eighty or so years, which is by no means fair.

"Rochelle, this has nothing to do with Queen Adair not returning Toren. In fact, she brought him here a few hours ago. Like we said earlier, there has been a complication," Elden stated, putting his hands up in a pacifying manner. "When Queen Adair and Toranthian returned to Earth, they didn't know that Sarina, Queen of the Vampires, was there waiting. Rochelle, before the Queen and Toranthian had a chance to react, she bit him."

Rochelle felt faint for a split second and her body swayed backwards. The wall of the building kept her upright and her eyes refocused on the men in front of her. "Is he dead, or one of them?" she asked, her voice void of emotion.

"He has become one of them," Elden answered. "I am sorry."

"Well, thank you both for coming and telling me in person. I will make sure to let the others know of his unfortunate set of circumstances. If you will both excuse me, I have a phantasm to take care of," she said, moving towards the door.

"Rochelle, there may be a way to save him," Manuel said. "We have come to ask for your help."

"What do you mean, save him? There is no cure for what he has been afflicted with."

"When Toranthian came to us after his accident, it was told to me by my Pegasus that he would be bitten by a vampire when he returned. I was told I wasn't allowed to interfere in the conversion process, as it was an event that was destined to occur, but my Pegasus' told me I could lessen the effects."

"Go on, Guardian Manuel. How can I save him?" Rochelle pleaded.

"We laced the broth that we fed him with a couple of doses of fairy dust. The Pegasus gave us the correct amount to add and told us we needed to find you. Is it true that you would do anything for him?" Guardian Manuel asked.

"Yes, I would die for him," Rochelle answered.

"Good, because you might just have to," Manuel replied. "There will be many years before you will have the opportunity to bring him back to what he once was, and you must add a pinch of this dust to your evening glass of water." Manuel handed her the container of dust.

"For how long?" she asked.

"Until you come face to face with your loved one, once more," Manuel answered.

"What happens when I run out?"

"You won't. I will be bringing a refill every couple of months until you no longer require it."

"And then what?" Rochelle queried.

"The Pegasus' do not tell us everything they see. Just what they need to pass on to ensure Destiny's will is fulfilled. All I know is that if you follow the Pegasus' advice, one day you might have the opportunity to save Toranthian from his vampirism. After that, who knows?"

Rochelle's phone rang. She pulled it out of her pocket and answered it.

"Rochelle, it's April. Have you got a minute?"

"It's April," she whispered to the Guardians while holding her hand over the mouthpiece.

"This conversation needs to remain between the three of us only," Elden whispered back.

Rochelle nodded her head in agreement. "Yeah, April, go ahead."

"Force and I would like to catch up with you later on this afternoon."

"April, I'm kinda busy here."

"Rochelle, it's important," April said with a sniffle.

"I know about Toren, April."

"I'm not calling about the helicopter crash," April assured her.

"No, you want to tell me Toren has become a vampire. I already know and I appreciate the fact you would like to tell me face-to-face. I'll be okay but I need some time on my own."

"Who told you?" April asked.

"It doesn't matter."

"Did you know Queen Adair was there?"

"Yes, I have been informed."

"She claims she couldn't stop Sarina from biting him."

"Yes, I heard that, too," Rochelle said angrily.

"I'm really sorry, Rochelle. We had a choice of letting him die, or finding him a human to feed off so the change could be successfully completed," April said.

"I'm glad you chose the latter. It is what I would have done, had I been there," Rochelle admitted. "April, I have to go. Thank you for being such a great friend. I will ring you in a few days once the situation has sunk in a bit more."

"If you need anything, please call."

"I will. I promise."

Rochelle hung up the phone and gave the Guardians an angry stare. "Queen Adair would have known immediately they stepped through the portal that Sarina was there. Why didn't she stop this?" Before he could stop himself, Elden thought about the ultimatum Sarina had given Adair and the ramifications that would have occurred if she had not given in to her demands. "Never mind, you just answered my question. I don't suppose you would take me to Mystique to see Toren and Sarina."

"That would be correct," Elden stated.

"One day, I am going to kill her."

"Who?" Manuel asked.

"Sarina, Queen of the Vampires," Rochelle stated.

"You can't kill her," Elden said. "Every vampire on Mystique is controlled by their maker, Sarina. If you kill her, we would have over one thousand vampires with a mind of their own."

"So?"

"Every Battle Star has the right DNA sequence to become a vampire once bitten. The only reason the vampires have not turned the Battle Stars already is because of an agreement that exists between Queen Adair and Sarina," Elden instructed.

"That is not entirely true," Manuel said carefully.

"What is not true?" Rochelle queried, barely holding on to her rage.

"If you kill Sarina, you kill Toren and all the other vampires made by her. It will be instantaneous and irreversible." Rochelle and Elden looked at him suspiciously. "It is true. Sarina believes the Queen would be more frightened by the thought of a thousand vampires on the rampage than the consequences she would face as a result of wiping out an entire species."

"I happen to agree with Sarina," Elden responded.

"Toren will not remain with her forever," Rochelle stated. "One day I will find a way to cure him and bring him home, to Earth."

"I certainly hope so."

"Thank you for the fairy dust. I will take it religiously. Please thank your Pegasus for the chance to save Toren from an eternity of vampirism," Rochelle said to Manuel.

"I will tell him, and I will see you in a couple of months with a new supply."

"Why can't I use some of our Locators' dust? It would be a lot easier."

"It needs to come from the fairy that provided the dust to Toren during his healing process," Elden said. "That fairy is staying on Mystique so that we can ensure her safety. You must not run out of dust, Rochelle. If you do, all hope is lost. There is one more thing, Toren gave this to Queen Adair as they stepped through the portal together," he said, handing her a small silver box with a dark blue ribbon. "The Queen asked me to make sure it was passed on to you."

Rochelle watched them walk through the gate and down the street. As soon as they had disappeared from view, she opened the box and her heart broke. Sitting on a bed of soft cotton, was a beautiful, diamond ring.

Her grief consumed her. She sank to the ground and curled up into the foetal position. She sobbed in despair as she thought about all of the things that she and Toren had seen and done together over the last five hundred years. As her misery deepened, water droplets suspended in the air gathered together to commiserate with her situation. But despair soon turned to fury, and the clouds darkened while sheets of lightning began blanketing the stratosphere.

Rochelle vowed she would not spend the rest of her life without him, and began plotting the ways she could pay Sarina back for the torment she had brought upon her, when their destinies intertwined together in the future. Lightning struck the ground several times before the Guardians realised Rochelle was capable of bringing a major catastrophe to the land.

"She is going to destroy the country if we don't do something!" Guardian Manuel yelled to be heard above the storm.

"What do you propose we do?" Guardian Elden asked. "Abduct her sister from America and bring her here?"

"That is an excellent idea. By the time we explain the situation the countryside could be gone." Manuel said as Elden opened a doorway.

"You do realise Chandra is even more volatile than Rochelle."

"What choice do we have?"

Elden contacted the Starlight Investigations crew and did a great job honing in on Chandra's location. He had brought them to a point that was directly behind her. Before she had time to register the difference in air pressure created by the portal, Manuel had wrapped his arms around her waist, pinning her arms tightly against her body.

She screamed in fright and threw her head backwards in an attempt to hurt her assailant, but the two of them had already begun falling through the portal. He hoped Elden wouldn't take too long to follow. The woman in his arms was seething with fury and, just like her sister, had full control over all of the elements. He needed to stay alive long enough to be able to explain the situation to Chandra and encourage her to help Rochelle deal with her loss before she destroyed the planet.

Titles by Marnie Atwell

Starlight Investigations

Jealousy Monsters

Vampire

Phantasm

Halloween Madness

The Pumpkin Patch

The House of Horrors

The Spirited Scarecrow

The Curious Kitten

About the Author

Marnie is an Australian author who lives in South-East Queensland with her husband and two children. When she is not dreaming up new adventures for her characters; Marnie enjoys writing, reading paranormal romance novels, and spending time with her family and friends. Not necessarily in that order.

Visit her website at: www.marnieatwell.com for more books, pictures, and downloads.

The next book in this series is:

Phantasm